Bess E. Miller Collection
of
Fairy Tales

Olive Fairy Book

Olive Fairy Book

collected and edited by

ANDREW LANG

illustrated by

ANNE VAUGHAN

with a foreword by

MARY GOULD DAVIS

DAVID McKAY COMPANY, INC.

New York

LANG

OLIVE FAIRY BOOK

FIRST EDITION SEPTEMBER 1907
NEW EDITION 1949
REPRINTED NOVEMBER 1950
NOVEMBER 1952
FEBRUARY 1965
JUNE 1967

Printed in the United States of America

VAN REES PRESS • NEW YORK

Foreword

MOST of the stories in the *Olive Fairy Book* come from India. Those that are from collections recorded in Turkey, Arabia, Armenia and the Sudan may have been brought from the Far East by people who came to settle in the Near East. Variants of a few of the stories may be found in collections like Flora Anna Steele's *Tales from the Punjab,* but for most of them the *Olive Fairy Book* is the only source.

In them all there is a touch of the Eastern philosophy, the wisdom and humor that belongs to the oldest of our civilizations. In each of them there is an idea that, as each little drama develops, becomes a part of the stream of consciousness of the children who read them, and so binds the West to the East. There is a likeness in many of them to the Sanskrit *Panchatantra* that, in Dr. Ryder's translation, has been such a challenge and such a treasure to modern storytellers. When the spark that the Ryder translation of *The Panchatantra* kindles is well a-light it will be wise to give this book to the children. With it they will go on to discover new plots, new characters and new ideas, in records that were old before the dawn of history in the Western world. Andrew Lang's fairy books have a way of telescoping time. Wali Dâd and The Snake Prince are as real today as they were when their stories were first told. Here is wit and wisdom that, old as it is, is ever new. This new edition of Andrew Lang's Eastern tales is a thread binding the present to the past, the ancient world to the world of tomorrow.

MARY GOULD DAVIS

August, 1948

Preface

MANY years ago my friend and publisher, Mr. Charles Long-
man, presented me with *Le Cabinet des Fées* (The Fairy
Cabinet). This work almost requires a swinging bookcase for
its accommodation, like the *Encyclopædia Britannica,* and in
a revolving bookcase I bestowed the volumes. Circumstances
of an intimately domestic character, 'not wholly unconnected,'
as Mr. Micawber might have said, with the narrowness of my
study (in which it is impossible to swing a cat) prevent the
revolving bookcase from revolving at this moment. I can see,
however, that the Fairy Cabinet contains at least forty volumes,
and I think there are about sixty in all.

This great plenitude of fairy tales from all quarters presents
legends of fairies, witches, geni or djinn, monsters, dragons,
wicked stepmothers, princesses, pretty or plain, princes lucky
or unlucky, giants, dwarfs, and enchantments. The stories
begin with those which children like best—the old 'Blue
Beard,' 'Puss in Boots,' 'Hop o' my Thumb,' 'Little Red Riding
Hood,' 'The Sleeping Beauty,' and 'Toads and Pearls.' These
were first collected, written, and printed at Paris in 1697. The
author was Monsieur Charles Perrault, a famous personage in
a great *perruque,* who in his day wrote large volumes now un-
read. He never dreamed that he was to be remembered mainly
by the shabby little volume with the tiny headpiece pictures.

Perrault picked up the rustic tales which the nurse of his
little boy used to tell, and he told them again in his own courtly,
witty way. They do not seem to have been translated into English until nearly thirty years later, when they were published
in English, with the French on the opposite page, by a Mr.

ix

Pote, a bookseller at Eton. Probably the younger Eton boys learned as much French as they condescended to acquire from these fairy tales, which are certainly more amusing than the *Télémaque* of Messire François de Salignac de la Motte-Fénelon, tutor of the children of France, Archbishop Duke of Cambrai, and Prince of the Holy Roman Empire.

The success of Perrault was based on the pleasure which the court of Louis XIV took in fairy tales; we know that they were told among court ladies from a letter of Madame de Sévigné. Naturally, Perrault had imitators, such as Madame d'Aulnoy, a wandering lady of more wit than reputation. To her we owe 'Beauty and the Beast' and 'The Yellow Dwarf.' Antony Hamilton tried his hand with 'The Ram,' a story too prolix and confused, best remembered for the remark, 'Ram, my friend, begin at the beginning!' Indeed, the narrative style of 'The Ram' is lacking in lucidity! Then came *The Arabian Nights,* translated by Monsieur Galland. Nobody has translated *The Arabian Nights* so well as Galland. His is the reverse of a scientific rendering, but it is as pleasantly readable as the *Iliad* and *Odyssey* would be if Alexandre Dumas had kept his promise to translate Homer. Galland omitted the verses and a great number of passages which nobody would miss, though the anthropologist is supposed to find them valuable and instructive in later scientific translations which do not amuse. Later, *Persian Tales, Tales of the Sea,* and original inventions, more or less on the fairy model, were composed by industrious men and women. They are far too long—are novels, indeed, and would please no child or mature person of taste. All these were collected in the vast Fairy Cabinet, published in 1786, just before the Revolution. Probably their attempt to be simple charmed a society which was extremely artificial, talked about 'the simple life' and the 'state of nature,' and was on the eve of a revolution in which human nature revealed her most primitive traits in orgies of blood.

That was the end of the court and of the court fairy tales, and just when they were demolished, learned men like the Grimms and Sir Walter Scott began to take an interest in the popular tales of peasants and savages all over the world. All the world over the tales were found to be essentially the same things. 'Cinderella' is everywhere; a whole book has been written on *Cinderella* by Miss Cox, and a very good book it is, but not interesting to children. For them the best of the collections of foreign fairy tales are the German stories by the Grimms, the *Tales from the Norse,* by Sir G. W. Dasent, (which some foolish grown-ups denounced as improper), and Miss Frere's Indian stories. There are hundreds of collections of savage and peasant fairy tales, but though many of these are most interesting, especially Bishop Callaway's Zulu stories (with the Zulu versions), these do not come in the way of parents and uncles, and therefore do not come in the way of children.

It is my wish that children should be allowed to choose their own books. Let their friends give them the money and turn them loose in the book shops! They know their own tastes, and if the children are born bookish, while their dear parents are the reverse (and this does occur), then the children make the better choice.

They are unaffected in their selections; some want Shakespeares of their own, and some prefer a volume entitled *Buster Brown.* A few—alas, how few—are fond of poetry; a still smaller number are fond of history. 'We know that there are no fairies, but history stories are true!' say these little innocents. I am not so sure there are no fairies, and I am only too well aware that the best history stories are not true.

What children do love are ghost stories. 'Tell us a ghost

story,' they cry, and I am able to meet the demand, with which I am in sincere sympathy. Only strong control prevents me from telling the last true ghost story which I heard yesterday. It would suit children excellently well. *The Grey Ghost Story Book* would be a favorite. At a very early age I read a number of advertisements of books and wept because I could not buy dozens of them, and somebody gave me a book on Botany! It looked all right, nicely bound in green cloth, but within it was full of all manner of tediousness.

In our Fairy Cabinet, which cannot extend to sixty volumes, we have aimed at pleasing children, not grown-ups, at whom the old French writers directed their romances, but have hunted for fairy tales in all quarters, not in Europe alone. In this volume we open, thanks to Dr. Ignas Künos, with a story from the Turks.

Major Campbell tells tales which he collected among the natives of India. But the sources are usually named at the end of each story, and when they are not named children will not miss them. Mrs. Lang, except in cases mentioned, has translated and adapted to the conditions of young readers the bulk of the collection. I must especially thank Monsieur Macler for permitting us to use some of his *Contes Arméniens* (Paris: Ernest Leroux, Editeur).

ANDREW LANG

Contents

Madschun . . . . **Page** 1

The Blue Parrot 10

A Long-bow Story 25

The Thanksgiving of the Wazir 30

Samba the Coward 36

Diamond Cut Diamond 46

The Five Wise Words 56

The Golden-headed Fish 66

Dorani 76

The Billy Goat and the King 85

Grasp All, Lose All 90

The Fate of the Turtle 99

The Snake Prince 105

The Clever Weaver 115

He Wins Who Waits 119

The Silent Princess 131

Jackal or Tiger? 150

Moti 165

Kupti and Imani 176

Wali Dâd the Simple-hearted 188

The Prince and the Three Fates 201

The Boy Who Found Fear 213

The Story of Zoulvisia 222

Illustrations

Color Plates

Frontispiece

Perceiving the swallow he knew help had come . Page   19

Suddenly there was nothing left but to surrender . . . 33

The palanquin was set down at Beeka Mull's shop . . 53

Dorani danced in the rajah's palace 81

The lady was joined by a young man 127

'O fairest of candlesticks, how are you?' 139

The princess summoned the king with a wave of her fan 181

Suddenly a fine stag started up 227

Black and White Plates

All the birds in the world nestle in its branches . . . 5

The princess dealt the horse a sharp cut 43

A hideous monster stepped noiselessly on to the rocks . 71

They dismounted in the shade to rest 87

Away and away flew the tree 97

At midnight the princess saw a snake wriggling along the
    floor 111

In the doorway appeared the beautiful girl 159

Moti dragged the tiger back to the serai 169

'O Allah! Here's a grand crowd coming!' 193

Down he went, down, down, down! 217

Olive Fairy Book

Madschun

ONCE UPON A TIME
there lived, in a small cottage among some hills, a woman
with her son. To her great grief, the young man, though
hardly more than twenty, had not as much hair on his head
as a baby. The youth was very idle, and to whatever trade his
mother put him he refused to work and in a few days always
came home again.

On a fine summer morning he was lying as usual half asleep
in the little garden in front of the cottage when the sultan's
daughter came riding by, followed by a number of gaily-
dressed ladies. The youth lazily raised himself on his elbow
to look at her, and that one glance changed his whole nature.

I will marry her and nobody else, he thought. And jumping up, he went to find his mother.

'You must go at once to the sultan and tell him that I want
his daughter for my wife,' he said.

'What!' shouted the old woman, shrinking back into a corner, for nothing but sudden madness could explain such an
amazing errand.

'Don't you understand? You must go at once to the sultan

and tell him that I want his daughter for my wife,' repeated the youth impatiently.

'But do you know what you are saying?' cried the mother. 'You will learn no trade and have only the five gold pieces left you by your father. Can you really expect that the sultan would give his daughter to a penniless baldpate like you?'

'That is my affair. Do as I ask you.' And neither day nor night did her son cease tormenting her, till in despair, she put on her best clothes, wrapped her veil about her, and went over the hill to the palace.

It was the day that the sultan set apart for hearing the complaints and petitions of his people, so the woman found no difficulty in gaining admission to his presence.

'Do not think me mad, O Excellency,' she began, 'but I have a son who, since his eyes have rested on the veiled face of the princess, has not left me in peace day or night till I consented to come to the palace, and to ask Your Excellency for your daughter's hand. It was in vain I answered that my head might pay the forfeit of my boldness, he would listen to nothing. Therefore am I here. Do with me even as you will!'

Now the sultan always loved anything out of the common, and this situation was new indeed. So instead of ordering the trembling creature to be flogged or cast into prison, as some sovereigns might have done, he merely said, 'Bid your son come hither.'

The old woman stared in astonishment at such a reply. But when the sultan repeated his words even more gently than before and did not look in anywise angered, she took courage, and bowing again she hastened homeward.

'Well, how have you sped?' asked her son eagerly as she crossed the threshold.

'You are to go up to the palace without delay and speak to the sultan himself,' replied the mother. And when he heard the good news, the son's face lightened up so wonderfully that his mother thought what a pity it was he had no hair, as then he would be quite handsome.

'Ah, the lightning will not fly more swiftly!' cried he. And in another instant he was out of her sight.

When the sultan beheld the bald head of his daughter's wooer, he no longer felt in the mood for joking, and resolved that somehow or other he must shake himself free of such an unwelcome suitor. But as he had summoned the young man to the palace, he could hardly dismiss him without a reason, so he hastily said:

'I hear you wish to marry my daughter. Well and good. But the man who is to be her husband must first collect all the birds in the world and bring them into the gardens of the palace, for hitherto no birds have made their homes in the trees.'

The young man was filled with despair at the sultan's words. How was he to snare all these birds? Even if he did succeed in catching them it would take years to carry them to the palace! Still, he was too proud to let the sultan think he had given up the princess without a struggle, so he took a road that led past the palace and walked on, not noticing whither he went.

So a week slipped by, and at length he found himself crossing a desert with great rocks scattered here and there. In the shadow cast by one of these was seated a holy man or dervish, as he was called, who motioned to the youth to sit beside him.

'Something is troubling you, my son,' said the holy man. 'Tell me what it is, for I may be able to help you.'

'Oh, my father,' answered the youth, 'I wish to marry the princess of my country, but the sultan refuses to give her to me unless I can collect all the birds in the world and bring them into his garden. How can I, or any other man, do that?'

'Do not despair,' replied the dervish, 'it is not so difficult as it sounds. Two days' journey from here, in the path of the setting sun, there stands a cypress tree, larger than any other cypress that grows upon the earth. Sit down where the shadow is darkest, close to the trunk, and keep very still. By-and-by you will hear a mighty rushing of wings and all the birds in the world will come and nestle in the branches.

'Be careful not to make a sound till everything is quiet again, and then say "Madschun!" At that the birds will be forced to remain where they are—not one can move from its perch, and you will be able to place them all over your head and arms and body, and in this way you must carry them to the sultan.'

With a glad heart the young man thanked the dervish and paid such close heed to his directions that, a few days later, a strange figure covered with soft feathers walked into the presence of the sultan. The princess' father was filled with surprise, for never had he seen such a sight before. Oh! How lovely were those little bodies and bright, frightened eyes!

All the birds in the world nestle in its branches

Soon a gentle stirring was heard and a multitude of wings unfolded themselves: blue wings, yellow wings, red wings, green wings. And when the young man whispered 'Go,' they first flew in circles round the sultan's head, then disappeared through the open window, to choose homes in the garden.

'I have done your bidding, O Sultan, and now give me the princess,' said the youth.

The sultan answered hurriedly, 'Yes! Oh, yes! You have pleased me well! Only one thing remains to turn you into a husband that any girl might desire. That head of yours—it is so very bald! Get it covered with nice thick curly hair, and then I will give you my daughter. You are so clever that I am sure this will give you no trouble at all.'

Silently the young man listened to the sultan's words and silently he sat in his mother's kitchen for many days to come, till, one morning, he heard that the sultan had betrothed his daughter to the son of the vizier. The wedding was to be celebrated without delay in the palace. With that he arose in wrath and, unseen by anyone, made his way into the mosque. Then he entered the palace by a gallery which opened straight into the great hall. Here the bride and bridegroom and two or three friends were assembled, waiting for the appearance of the sultan for the contract to be signed.

'Madschun!' whispered the youth from above, and instantly everyone remained rooted to the ground. Some messengers whom the sultan had sent to see that all was ready shared the same fate.

At length, angry and impatient, the sultan went down to behold with his own eyes what had happened. As nobody could give him any explanation, he bade one of his attendants fetch a magician to remove the spell cast by some evil genius.

'It is your own fault,' said the magician, when he had heard the sultan's story. 'If you had not broken your promise to the young man, your daughter would not have had this ill befall her. Now there is only one remedy and the bridegroom you have chosen must yield his place to the bald-headed youth.'

Sore though he was in his heart, the sultan knew the magician was wiser than he, and dispatched his most trusted servants to seek out the young man without a moment's delay and bring him to the palace. The youth, who all this time had been hiding behind a pillar, smiled to himself.

Hastening home, he said to his mother, 'If messengers from the sultan should ask for me, be sure you answer that it is a long while since I went away, and that you cannot tell where I may be, but if they will give you money enough for your journey, as you are very poor, you will do your best to find me.'

Then he hid himself in the loft above, so he could listen to all that passed. The next minute someone knocked loudly at the door, and the old woman jumped up and opened it.

'Is your bald-headed son here?' asked the man outside. 'If so, let him come with me, for the sultan wishes to speak with him directly.'

'Alas, sir,' replied the woman, putting a corner of her veil to her eyes, 'he left me long ago and since that day no news of him has reached me.'

'Oh, good lady, can you not guess where he may be? The sultan intends to bestow on him the hand of his daughter, and he is certain to give a large reward to the man who brings him back.'

'He never told me whither he was going,' answered the crone, shaking her head. 'But it is a great honor the sultan does him, and well worth some trouble. There are places where, perhaps, he may be found, but they are known only to me. But I am a poor woman and have no money for the journey.'

'Oh, that will not stand in the way!' cried the man. 'In this purse are a thousand gold pieces; spend them freely. Tell me where I can find him and you shall have as many more.'

'Very well,' said she, 'it is a bargain; and now farewell, for I must make some preparations. In a few days at furthest you shall hear from me.'

For nearly a week both the old woman and her son were careful not to leave the house till it was dark, lest they should be seen by any of the neighbors. As they did not even kindle a fire or light a lantern, everyone supposed that the cottage was deserted. At length, one fine morning, the young man rose early, dressed, and put on his best turban. Then, after a hasty breakfast, he took the road to the palace.

The huge Negro before the door evidently expected him, for without a word he let him pass, and another attendant who was waiting inside conducted him straight into the presence of the sultan, who welcomed him gladly.

'Ah, my son, where have you hidden yourself all this time?' said he.

And the bald-headed man answered, 'Oh, Sultan! Fairly I won your daughter, but you broke your word and would not give her to me. Then my home grew hateful to me and I set out to wander through the world! But now that you have repented of your ill-faith, I have come to claim the wife who is mine of right. Therefore bid your vizier prepare the contract.'

So a fresh contract was prepared and, at the wish of the new bridegroom, was signed by the sultan and the vizier in the chamber where they met. After this was done, the youth begged the sultan to lead him to the princess, and together they entered the great hall, where everyone was standing exactly as they were when the young man had uttered the fatal word.

'Can you remove the spell?' asked the sultan anxiously.

'I think so,' replied the young man who, to say the truth, was a little anxious himself. Stepping forward, he cried, 'Let the victims of Madschun be free!'

No sooner were the words uttered than the statues returned to life, and the bride placed her hand joyfully in that of her new bridegroom. As for the old one, he vanished completely, and no one ever knew what became of him.

[Adapted from *Türkische Volksmärchen aus Stambul*. Dr. Ignas Künos. E. J. Brill. Leiden.]

The Blue Parrot

IN A PART OF ARABIA
where groves of palms and sweet-scented flowers give the traveler rest after toilsome journeys under burning skies, there reigned a young king whose name was Lino. He had grown up under the wise rule of his father, who had lately died, and though he was only nineteen, he did not believe, like many young men, that he must change all the laws in order to show how clever he was, but was content with the old ones which had made the people happy and the country prosperous. There was only one fault his subjects had to find with him: he did not seem in any hurry to be married, in spite of their prayers.

The neighboring kingdom was governed by the Swan Fairy, who had an only daughter, the Princess Hermosa, as charming in her way as Lino in his. The Swan Fairy's ambassador at the young king's court hearing the grumbles of the citizens resolved that he would try his hand at matchmaking.

'For,' he said, 'if there is anyone living who is worthy of the Princess Hermosa he is to be found here. At any rate, I can but try and bring them together.'

Now, of course, it was not proper to offer the princess in marriage, and the difficulty was to work upon the king so the proposal would come from him. But the ambassador was well used to the ways of courts, and after several conversations on the art of painting, which Lino loved, he led the talk to portraits and mentioned carelessly that a particularly fine picture had lately been made of his own princess.

'Though, as for a likeness,' he concluded, 'perhaps it is hardly as good as this small miniature, which was painted a year ago.'

The king took it, and looked at it closely. 'Ah,' he sighed, 'that must be flattering! It cannot be possible that any woman should be such a miracle of beauty.'

'If you could only see her,' answered the ambassador.

The king did not reply, but the ambassador was not at all surprised when, the following morning, he was ushered into the royal presence.

'Since you showed me that picture,' Lino said, almost before the door was shut, 'I have not been able to banish the face of the princess from my thoughts. I have summoned you here to inform you that I am about to send special envoys to the court of the Swan Fairy, asking her daughter in marriage.'

'I cannot, as you will understand, speak for my mistress in so important a matter,' replied the ambassador, stroking his beard in order to conceal the satisfaction he felt. 'But I know she will certainly be highly gratified at your proposal.'

'If that is so,' cried the king, his whole face beaming with joy, 'then, instead of sending envoys, I will go myself and take you with me. In three days my preparations will be made, and we will set out.'

UNLUCKILY for Lino, he had for his neighbor on the other side a powerful magician named Ismenor. He was King of the Isle of Lions, and the father of a hideous daughter, whom he thought the most beautiful creature that ever existed. Riquette, for such was her name, had also fallen in love with a portrait, but it was of King Lino, and she implored her father to give him to her for a husband.

Ismenor, who considered that no man lived who was worthy of his treasure, was about to send his chief minister to King Lino, when he heard that the king had already started for the court of the Swan Fairy. Riquette was thrown into transports of grief and implored her father to prevent the marriage, which Ismenor promised to do. Calling for an ugly little groom named Rabot, he performed some spells which transported them quickly to a rocky valley through which the king and his escort were bound to pass.

When the tramp of horses was heard, the magician took out an enchanted handkerchief, which rendered invisible anyone who touched it. Giving one end to Rabot and holding the other himself, they walked unseen amongst the horsemen, but not a trace of Lino was to be found. And this was natural enough, because the king, tired out with the excitement and fatigue of the last few days, had bidden the heavy coaches, laden with presents for the princess, to go forward while he rested under the palms with a few of his friends. Here Ismenor beheld them, all sound asleep. Casting a spell, which prevented their waking till he wished them to do so, he stripped the king of all his clothes and dressed him in those of Rabot, whom he touched with his ring, saying:

'Take the shape of Lino until you have wedded the daughter of the Swan Fairy.'

And so great was the magician's power that Rabot believed himself to be really the king!

When the groom had mounted Lino's horse and ridden out of sight, Ismenor aroused the king, who stared with astonishment at his dirty garments. But before he had time to

look about him, the magician caught Lino up in a cloud and carried him off to his daughter.

Meanwhile Rabot had come up with the others, who never guessed for a moment he was not their own master. 'I am hungry,' said he, 'give me something to eat at once.'

'May it please Your Majesty,' answered the steward, 'the tents are not even set up, and it will be at least an hour before your supper is served! We thought—'

'Who taught you to think?' interrupted the false king rudely. 'You are nothing but a fool! Get me some horse flesh directly —it is the best meat in the world!'

The steward could hardly believe his ears. King Lino, the most polite man under the sun, to speak to his faithful servant in such a manner! And to want horse flesh too! Why, his appetite was so delicate he lived mostly on fruit and cakes. Well, well, there was no knowing what people would come to; and, anyhow, he must obey at once, if he wished to keep his head on his shoulders. Perhaps love had driven the king mad, and if so, by-and-by he might come right again.

Whatever excuses his old servants might invent for their master, by the time the procession reached the Swan Fairy's capital there were no more horses left, and they were forced to walk up to the palace on foot. They soon perceived the Swan Fairy and her daughter awaiting them on a low balcony, under which the king stopped.

'Madam,' he said, 'you may be surprised that I have come to ask your daughter's hand in so unceremonious a fashion; but the journey is long, and I was hungry and ate the horses, which is the best meat in the world. But for all that I am a great king, and wish to be your son-in-law. And now that is settled, where is Hermosa?'

'Sire,' answered the queen, not a little displeased as well as

'Control yourself, my child,' said the fairy. 'We have need [of] all our wits if we are to rescue the king from the power [of] those wicked people. First of all it is necessary to know [w]ho the man that has taken his name and his face really is.'

Then, picking up the mirror, she wished that she might [b]ehold the false lover. The glass gave back a vision of a dirty, [g]reasy groom lying, dressed as he was, on her bed of state.

'So this is the trick Ismenor hoped to play us! Well, we will [h]ave our revenge, whatever it costs us to get it. Only we must [b]e very careful not to let him guess that he has not deceived [u]s, for his skill in magic is greater than mine, and I shall have [t]o be very prudent. To begin with, I must leave you, and if the [f]alse king asks why, then answer that I have to settle some affairs on the borders of my kingdom. Meanwhile, be sure you treat him most politely and arrange fêtes to amuse him. If he shows any sign of being suspicious, you can even give him to understand that, on your marriage, I intend to give up the crown to your husband. And now, farewell!'

So saying, the Swan Fairy waved her hand, and a cloud came down and concealed her. Nobody imagined the beautiful amazed at the king's manner, which was so different from anything she had been led to expect. 'You possess my daughter's portrait, and it can have made but little impression on you if you do not recognize her at once.'

'I don't remember any portrait,' replied Rabot, 'but perhaps it may be in my pocket after all.' And he searched everywhere, while the ladies-in-waiting looked on with astonishment, but of course he found nothing. Then he turned to the princess, who stood there blushing and angry, and said:

'If it is you I have come to marry, I suppose you are very beautiful. I am sure if I had seen your portrait I should have remembered it. Let us have the wedding as soon as possible. In the meantime, I should like to go to sleep; I can assure you that after walking over stones and sand for days and days one needs a little rest.'

And without waiting for a reply he bade one of the pages conduct him to his room. Soon he was snoring so loud that he could be heard at the other end of the town.

When he was out of their sight the poor princess flung herself into her mother's arms and burst into tears. For fifteen days she had had King Lino's portrait constantly before her, while the letter from their own ambassador speaking of the young man's grace and charm had never left her pocket. True, the portrait was faithful enough, but how could that fair outside contain so rough and rude a soul? Yet even this she might have forgiven had the king shown any of the signs of love and admiration to which she had been so long accustomed. As for her mother, the poor Swan Fairy was so bewildered at the extraordinary manners of Lino that she was almost speechless.

Matters were in this state when King Lino's chamberlain begged for a private audience of her majesty. No sooner were they alone than he told her he feared that his master had sud-

denly gone mad or had fallen under the spell

'I had been lost in astonishment before,' that he has failed to recognize the princes possesses her portrait, from which he never for a single instant, my amazement knows no madam, your fairy gifts may discover the reaso in one whose courtesy was the talk of the king a low bow he took his departure.

The queen stood thinking deeply. Suddenly and going to an old chest, which she kept in she drew from it a small mirror. In this mirro faithfully reflected whatever she wished, and she desired above all things to behold King Li was.

Ah, the chamberlain was right! It was not Li his bed, snoring till the whole palace shook ben he was the man dressed in dirty clothes, impriso Ismenor's strongest towers, and kissing the portrai which had escaped the wizard's notice.

Calling hastily to her daughter, she bade her Hermosa had the pleasure of gazing on Lino, having exactly as she could have wished. The mi in her hand when the door of the prison opene entered the hideous Riquette who, from her u seemed to be begging from Lino some favor whic to grant. Of course Hermosa and her mother cou their words, but from Riquette's angry face as room, it was not difficult to guess what had happ

But the mirror had more to tell. In fury at her reje king, Riquette ordered four strong men to scourg he fainted. Hermosa in horror dropped the mirror, have fallen had she not been caught by her mother.

white cloud, blown so rapidly across the sky, was the chariot carrying the Swan Fairy to the tower of Ismenor.

Now the tower was situated in the midst of a forest, so the queen thought that, under cover of the dark trees, it would be quite easy for her to drop to earth unseen. But the tower was so thoroughly enchanted that the more she tried to reach the ground the tighter something tried to hold her back. At length, by putting forth all her power, she managed to descend to the foot of the tower.

There, weak and faint as she was with her exertions, she lost no time in working her spells, and found that she could only overcome Ismenor by means of a stone from the ring of Gyges. But how was she to get this ring? For the magic book told her that Ismenor guarded it night and day among his most precious treasures. However, get it she must, and in the meantime the first step was to see the royal prisoner himself. So, drawing out her tablets, she wrote as follows:

The bird which brings you this letter is the Swan Fairy, mother of Hermosa, who loves you as much as you love her! And after this assurance, she related the wicked plot of which he had been the victim. Then, quickly changing herself into a swallow, she began to fly round the tower till she discovered the window of Lino's prison. It was so high up that bars seemed needless, especially as four soldiers were stationed in the passage outside, therefore the fairy was able to enter, and even to hop on his shoulder, but Lino was gazing so steadily at the princess' portrait it was some time before she could attract his attention.

At last she gently scratched his cheek with the corner of the note, and he looked round with a start. On perceiving the swallow he knew at once that help had come. Tearing open the letter, he wept with joy on seeing the words it contained and asked a thousand questions as to Hermosa, which the swallow was unable to answer, though, by repeated nods, she signed to him to read further.

'Must I indeed pretend to wish to marry that horrible Riquette?' he cried, when he had finished. 'Can I obtain the stone from the magician?'

Accordingly, the next morning, when Riquette paid him her daily visit, he received her more graciously than usual. The magician's daughter could not contain her delight at this change. In answer to her expressions of joy, Lino told her of a dream by which he had learned the inconstancy of Hermosa; also that a fairy had appeared and informed him that if he wished to break the bonds which bound him to the faithless princess and transfer his affections to the daughter of Ismenor, he must have in his possession for a day and a night a stone from the ring of Gyges.

This news so enchanted Riquette that she flung her arms round the king's neck and embraced him tenderly, greatly to his disgust, as he would infinitely have preferred the sticks of the soldiers. However, there was no help for it, and he did his best to seem pleased, till Riquette relieved him by announcing that she must lose no time in asking her father and obtaining from him the precious stone.

His daughter's request came as a great surprise to Ismenor, whose suspicions were instantly excited; but, think as he would, he could see no means by which the king, so closely guarded, might have held communication with the Swan Fairy. Still, he would do nothing hastily, and hiding his dismay, he told Riquette that his only wish was to make her happy, and as she wished so much for the stone he would fetch it for her. Then he went into the closet where all his spells were worked,

Perceiving the swallow he knew help had come

and in a short time he discovered that his enemy the Swan Fairy was at that moment inside his palace.

'So that is it!' he said, smiling grimly. 'Well, she shall have a stone by all means, but a stone that will turn anyone who touches it into marble.' And placing a small ruby in a box, he returned to his daughter.

'Here is the talisman which will gain you the love of King Lino,' he said, 'but be sure you give him the box unopened, else the stone will lose all its virtue.'

With a cry of joy Riquette snatched the box from his hands and ran off to the prison, followed by her father who, holding the enchanted handkerchief, was able, unseen, to watch the working of the spell. As he expected, at the foot of the tower stood the Swan Fairy, imprudently in her natural shape, waiting for the stone which the prince was to throw to her. Eagerly she caught the box as it fell from the prince's hands, but no sooner had her fingers touched the ruby, than a curious hardening came over her, her limbs stiffened, and her tongue could hardly utter the words, 'We are betrayed.'

'Yes, you are betrayed,' cried Ismenor, in a terrible voice. 'And you,' he continued, dragging the king to the window, 'you shall turn into a parrot, and a parrot you will remain until you can persuade Hermosa to crush in your head.'

He had hardly finished before a blue parrot flew out into the forest. The magician, mounting in his winged chariot, set off for the Isle of Swans, where he changed everybody into statues, exactly in the positions in which he found them, not even excepting Rabot himself. Only Hermosa was spared, and her he ordered to get into his chariot beside him.

In a few minutes he reached the Forest of Wonders, where the magician got down and dragged the unhappy princess out after him.

'I have changed your mother into a stone and your lover into a parrot,' said he, 'and you are to become a tree. A tree you will remain until you have crushed the head of the person you love best in the world. But I will leave you your mind and memory that your tortures may be increased a thousand-fold'

Great magician as he was, Ismenor could not have invented a more terrible fate had he tried for a hundred years. The hours passed wearily by for the poor princess, who longed for a woodcutter's axe to put an end to her misery. How were they to be delivered from their doom? And even supposing that King Lino did fly that way, there were thousands of blue parrots in the forest, and how was she to know him, or he her? And her mother—ah, that was too sad to think about! So, being a woman, she kept on thinking.

Meanwhile, the blue parrot flew about the world till, one day, he entered the castle of an old wizard who had just married a beautiful young wife. Grenadine, for such was her name, led a very dull life and was delighted to have a playfellow, so she gave the parrot a golden cage to sleep in and delicious fruits to eat. Only in one way did he disappoint her—he never would talk as other parrots did.

'If you only knew how happy it would make me, I'm sure you would try,' she was fond of saying; but the parrot did not seem to hear her.

One morning, however, the parrot, finding himself alone, hopped to the table and, picking up a pencil, wrote some verses on a piece of paper. He was startled by a noise and, letting fall the pencil, flew out of the window.

Now hardly had he dropped the pencil when the wizard lifted a corner of the curtain which hung over the doorway and advanced into the room. Seeing a paper on the table he picked it up, and great was his surprise as he read:

Fair princess, to win your grace,
I will hold discourse with you;
Silence, though, were more in place
Than chatt'ring like a cockatoo.

'I half suspected it was enchanted,' murmured the wizard
to himself. And he fetched his books and searched them and
found that, instead of being a parrot, the bird was really a king
who had fallen under the wrath of a magician, and that magician the man whom the wizard hated most in the world.

Eagerly he read on, seeking for some means of breaking
the enchantment, and at last, to his great joy, he discovered the
remedy. Then he hurried to his wife and informed her that
her favorite was really the king of a great country, and that,
if she would whistle for the bird, they would all go together to
a certain spot in the Forest of Wonders. 'There I will restore
him to his own shape. Only you must not be afraid or cry out,
whatever I do,' he added, 'or everything will be spoiled.'

The wizard's wife jumped up in an instant, so delighted
was she, and began to whistle the song the parrot loved. But
as he did not wish it to be known he had been listening to the
conversation he waited until she had turned her back, when
he flew down from the tree and alighted on her shoulder. Then
they stepped into a golden boat, which carried them to a clear-
ing in the forest, where three tall trees stood by themselves.

'I want these trees for my magic fire,' the wizard said to his
wife. 'Put the parrot on that branch; he will be quite safe, and
go yourself to a little distance. If you stay too near you may
get your head crushed in their fall.'

At these words the parrot suddenly remembered the prophecy
of Ismenor and held himself ready, his heart beating at the
thought that in one of those trees was Hermosa. Meanwhile

the wizard took a spade and loosened the earth at the roots of
the three trees so they might fall all together. The parrot saw
them totter, spread his wings, and flew right under the middle
one, which was the most beautiful of the three. There was a
crash, then Lino and Hermosa stood facing each other, clasped
hand in hand.

After the first few moments, the princess' thoughts turned
to her mother, and falling at the feet of the wizard, who was
smiling with delight at the success of his plan, she implored
him to help them once more and to give the Swan Fairy back
her proper shape.

'That is not so easy,' said he, 'but I will try what I can do.'
And transporting himself to his palace to obtain a little bottle
of magic water, he waited till nightfall, and started at once
for Ismenor's tower. Of course, had Ismenor consulted his
books he would have seen what his enemy was doing and
might have protected himself; but he had been eating and
drinking too much and was sleeping heavily. Changing himself into a bat, the wizard flew into the room, and poured the
magic liquid over Ismenor's face so he died without a

groan. At the same instant the Swan Fairy became a woman again, for no magician, however powerful, can work spells which last beyond his own life.

So when the Swan Fairy returned to her capital she found all her courtiers waiting at the gate to receive her, and in their midst, beaming with happiness, Hermosa and King Lino. Standing behind them, though a long way off, was Rabot; but his dirty clothes had given place to clean ones, when his earnest desire was granted, and the princess had made him head of her stables.

And here we must bid them all farewell, feeling sure they will have many years of happiness before them after the terrible trials through which they have passed.

[Adapted and shortened from *Le Cabinet des Fées*.]

A Long-Bow Story

ONE DAY A BUNNIAH, or banker and grain merchant, was walking along a country road when he overtook a farmer going in the same direction. Now the bunniah was very grasping, and was lamenting that he had not had a chance of making any money that day; but at the sight of the man in front he brightened up wonderfully.

'That is a piece of luck,' he said to himself. 'Let me see if this farmer is not good for something.' And he hastened his steps.

After they had bid each other good day very politely, the bunniah said to the farmer, 'I was just thinking how dull I felt, when I beheld you, but since we are going the same way, I shall find the road quite short in such agreeable company.'

'With all my heart,' replied the farmer. 'But what shall we talk about? A city man like you will not care to hear about cattle and crops.'

'Oh,' said the bunniah, 'I'll tell you what we will do. We will each tell the other the wildest tale we can imagine, and he who first throws doubt on the other's story shall pay him a hundred rupees.'

To this the farmer agreed and begged the bunniah to begin, as he was the bigger man of the two. Privately he made up his

mind that, however improbable it might be, nothing should induce him to hint that he did not believe in the bunniah's tale. Thus politely pressed the great man started:

'I was going along this road one day, when I met a merchant traveling with a great train of camels laden with merchandise—'

'Very likely,' murmured the farmer; 'I've seen that kind of thing myself.'

'No less than one hundred and one camels,' continued the bunniah, 'all tied together by their nose strings—nose to tail—and stretching along the road for almost half a mile—'

'Well?' said the farmer.

'Well, a kite swooped down on the foremost camel and bore him off, struggling, into the air, and by reason of them all being tied together the other hundred camels had to follow—'

'Amazing, the strength of that kite!' said the farmer. 'But—yes, doubtless; yes—well—one hundred and one camels—And what did he do with them?'

'You doubt it?' demanded the bunniah.

'Not a bit!' said the farmer heartily.

'Well,' continued the bunniah, 'it happened that the princess of a neighboring kingdom was sitting in her private garden, having her hair combed by her maid, and she was looking upward, with her head thrown back, while the maid tugged away at the comb, when that wretched kite with its prey went soaring overhead. As luck would have it, the camels gave an extra kick just then, the kite lost his hold, and the whole hundred and one camels dropped right into the princess' left eye!'

'Poor thing!' said the farmer. 'It's so painful having anything in one's eye.'

'Well,' said the bunniah, who was now warming to his task, 'the princess shook her head and sprang up, clapping her hand to her eye. "Oh, dear!" she cried. "I've got something in my eye and how it does smart!" '

'It always does,' observed the farmer, 'perfectly true. Well, what did the poor thing do?'

'At the sound of her cries, the maid came running to her assistance. "Let me look," said she; and with that she gave the princess' eyelid a twitch, and out came a camel, which the maid put in her pocket—' ('Ah!' grunted the farmer)—'and then she just twisted up the corner of her headcloth and fished a hundred more of them out of the princess' eye and popped them all into her pocket with the other.'

Here the bunniah gasped as one who is out of breath, but the farmer looked at him slowly. 'Well?' said he.

'I can't think of anything more now,' replied the bunniah. 'Besides, that is the end; what do you say to it?'

'Wonderful,' replied the farmer, 'and no doubt perfectly true!'

'Well, it is your turn,' said the bunniah. 'I am so anxious to hear your story. I am sure it will be very interesting.'

'Yes, I think it will,' answered the farmer, and he began:

'My father was a very prosperous man. Five cows he had and three yoke of oxen and half a dozen buffaloes and goats in abundance; but of all his possessions the thing he loved best was a mare. A well-bred mare she was—oh, a very fine mare!'

'Yes, yes,' interrupted the bunniah, 'get on!'

'I'm getting on,' said the farmer, 'don't you hurry me! Well, one day, as ill-luck would have it, he rode that mare to market with a torn saddle, which galled her so that when they returned home she had a sore on her back as big as the palm of your hand.'

'Yes,' said the bunniah impatiently, 'what next?'

'It was June,' said the farmer, 'and you know how, in June, the air is full of dust storms with rain at times? Well, the poor beast got dust in that wound, and what's more, with the dust some grains of wheat. And, what with the dust and the heat and the wet, that wheat sprouted and began to grow!'

'Wheat does when it gets a fair chance,' said the bunniah.

'Yes, and the next thing we knew there was a crop of wheat on that mare's back as big as anything you ever saw in a hundred-acre field, and we had to hire twenty men to reap it!'

'One generally has to hire extra hands for reaping,' said the bunniah.

'And we got four hundred maunds of wheat off that mare's back!' continued the farmer.

'A good crop!' murmured the bunniah.

'And your father,' said the farmer, 'a poor wretch, with hardly enough to keep body and soul together—(the bunniah snorted, but was silent)—came to my father, and he said, putting his hands together as humble as could be—'

The bunniah here flashed a furious glance at his companion, but bit his lips and held his peace.

' "I haven't tasted food for a week. Oh, great master, let me have the loan of sixteen maunds of wheat from your store, and I will repay you." '

' "Certainly, neighbor," answered my father; "take what you need and repay it as you can." '

'Well?' demanded the bunniah with fury in his heart.

'Well, he took the wheat away with him,' replied the farmer; 'but he never repaid it, and it's a debt to this day. Sometimes I wonder whether I shall not go to law about it.'

Then the bunniah began running his thumb quickly up and down the fingers of his right hand, and his lips moved in quick calculation.

'What is the matter?' asked the farmer.

'The wheat is the cheaper; I'll pay you for the wheat,' said the bunniah, with the calmness of despair, as he remembered that by his own arrangement he was bound to give the farmer a hundred rupees.

And to this day they say in those parts, when a man owes a debt: 'Give me the money; or, if not that, give me at least the wheat.'

[This is from oral tradition.]

The Thanksgiving of the Wazir

ONCE UPON A TIME
there lived in Hindustan two kings whose countries bordered
upon each other; but, as they were rivals in wealth and power,
and one was a Hindu rajah and the other a Mohammedan
bâdshah, they were not good friends at all. To escape continual
quarrels, the rajah and the bâdshah had drawn up an agreement, stamped and signed, declaring that if any of their subjects, from the least to the greatest, crossed the boundary between the two kingdoms, he might be seized and punished.

One morning the bâdshah and his chief wazir, or prime
minister, were at work over the affairs of the kingdom. The
bâdshah had taken up a pen and was cutting it to his liking
with a sharp knife, when the knife slipped and cut off the tip
of his finger.

'Oh-he, Wazir!' cried the king. 'I've cut the tip of my finger
off!'

'That is good hearing!' said the wazir in answer.

'Insolent one,' exclaimed the king. 'Do you take pleasure in
the misfortunes of others and in mine also? Take him away,

my guards, and put him in the court prison until I have time to punish him as he deserves!'

Instantly the officers in attendance seized upon the luckless wazir and dragged him out of the king's presence toward the narrow doorway, through which unhappy criminals were wont to be led to prison or execution. As the door opened to receive him, the wazir muttered something into his great white beard which the soldiers could barely hear.

'What said the rascal?' shouted the angry king.

'He says he thanks Your Majesty,' replied one of the gaolers. And at his words, the king stared at the closing door, in anger and amazement.

'He must be mad,' he cried, 'for he is grateful, not only for the misfortunes of others, but for his own. Surely something has turned his head!'

Now the king was very fond of his old wazir, and although the court physician came and bound up his injured finger with cool and healing ointment and soothed the pain, he could not soothe the soreness of the king's heart, nor could any of all his ministers and courtiers, who found his majesty very cross all the day long.

Early next morning the king ordered his horse and declared he would go hunting. Instantly all was bustle and preparation in stable and hall, and soon a score of ministers and huntsmen stood ready to mount and accompany him. To their astonishment the king would have none of them. Indeed, he glared at them so fiercely they were glad to leave him. So away and away he wandered, over field and through forest, so moody and thoughtful that many a fat buck and gaudy pheasant escaped.

So careless was he that he strayed without perceiving it over into the rajah's territory. Suddenly, men stepped from all sides out of the thickets, and there was nothing left but surrender. Then the poor bâdshah was seized and bound and taken to the rajah's prison, thinking most of the time of his wazir, who was suffering a similar fate, and wishing that, like the wazir, he could feel thankful.

That night the rajah held a special council to consider what should be done to his rival who had thus given himself into his hands. All the Brahmans were sent for and, while all the rest of the rajah's councilors were offering him different advice until he was nearly crazy with anger and indecision, the chief Brahman was squatting in a corner, figuring out sums and signs to himself, with an admiring group of lesser ones around him. At last he rose and advanced toward the throne.

'Well,' said the rajah anxiously, 'what have you to advise?'

'A very unlucky day!' exclaimed the chief Brahman. 'Oh, a very unlucky day! The god Devi is full of wrath and commands that tomorrow you must chop off this bâdshah's head and offer it to him in sacrifice.'

'Ah, well,' said the rajah, 'let it be done. I leave it to you to carry out the sentence.' And he bowed to him and left the room.

Before dawn great preparations were being made for a grand festival in honor of the great idol Devi. Hundreds of banners waved, hundreds of drummers drummed, hundreds of singers chanted, hundreds of priests, well washed and anointed, performed their sacred rites, while the rajah sat, nervous and ill at ease, among hundreds of courtiers and servants, wishing it were all well over. At last the time came for the sacrifice to be offered, and the poor bâdshah was bound and led out to have his head chopped off.

The chief Brahman came along with a smile on his face, a big sword in his hand. Suddenly, he noticed that the bâdshah's

Suddenly there was nothing left but to surrender

finger was tied up in a bit of rag. Instantly he dropped the sword and, with his eyes starting out of his head with excitement, pounced upon the rag and tore it off, and saw that the tip of his victim's finger was missing. At this he was very angry indeed, and he led the bâdshah up to where the rajah sat wondering.

'Behold! O Rajah,' he said, 'this sacrifice is useless, the tip of his finger is gone! A sacrifice is no sacrifice unless it is complete.' And he began to weep with rage and mortification.

But instead of wailing likewise, the rajah gave a sigh of relief, and answered, 'Well, that settles the matter. If it had been anyone else I should not have minded, but somehow it doesn't seem quite right to sacrifice a king.' And with that he jumped up and with his jeweled dagger cut the bâdshah's cords and marched with him out of the temple back to the palace.

After having bathed and refreshed his guest, the rajah loaded him with gifts, and himself accompanied him with a large escort as far as the frontier between their kingdoms, where, amidst salutes and great rejoicings, they tore up the old agreement and drew up another in which each king promised welcome and safe conduct to any of the other's people, from the least to the greatest, who came over the border on any errand whatsoever. And so they embraced, and each went his own way.

When the bâdshah reached home that evening he sent for his imprisoned wazir.

'Well, O Wazir,' he said, when the old man had been brought before him, 'what think you has been happening to me?'

'How can a man in prison know what is happening outside it?' answered the wazir.

Then the bâdshah told him all his adventures. And when he had reached the end he added:

'I have made up my mind, as a token of gratitude for my escape, to pardon you freely, if you will tell me why you gave thanks when I cut off the tip of my finger.'

'Sire,' replied the old wazir, 'am I not right in thinking that it was a very lucky thing for you that you did cut off the tip of your finger, for otherwise you would certainly have lost your head. And to lose a scrap of one's finger is surely the least of the two evils.'

'Very true,' answered the king, touching his head as he spoke, as if to make quite certain it was still there, 'but yet—why did you likewise give thanks when I put you into prison?'

'I gave thanks,' said the wazir, 'because it is good always to give thanks. And had I known that my being in prison was to prevent the god Devi claiming me instead of Your Majesty, as a perfect offering, I should have given greater thanks still.'

[Punjâbi story.]

Samba the Coward

IN THE GREAT COUNTRY far away south, through which flows the river Nile, there lived a king who had an only child called Samba.

Now, from the time Samba could walk he showed signs of being afraid of everything, and as he grew bigger he became more and more frightened. At first his father's friends made light of it and said to one another:

'It is strange to see a boy of our race running into a hut at the trumpeting of an elephant, and trembling with fear if a lion cub half his size comes near him. But, after all, he is only a baby, and when he is older he will be as brave as the rest.'

'Yes, he is only a baby,' answered the king who overheard them; 'it will be all right by-and-by.' But, somehow, he sighed as he said it, and the men looked at him and made no reply.

The years passed away, and Samba had become a tall and strong youth. He was good-natured and pleasant and was liked by all, and if during his father's hunting parties he was seldom to be seen in any place of danger, he was too great a favorite for much to be said.

'When the king holds the feast and declares him to be his heir, he will cease to be a child,' murmured the people, as they

had done before. And on the day of the ceremony their hearts
beat gladly, and they cried to one another:

'It is Samba, Samba, whose chin is above the heads of other
men, who will defend us against the tribes of the robbers!'

Not many weeks after, the dwellers in the village awoke
to find that during the night their herds had been driven
away, and their herdsmen carried off into slavery. Now was
the time for Samba to show the brave spirit that had come to
him with his manhood and to ride forth at the head of the
warriors of his race. But Samba could nowhere be found, and
a party of avengers went on their way without him.

It was many days later before he came back, with his head
held high, and a tale of a lion which he had tracked to its lair
and killed, at the risk of his own life. A little while earlier and
his people would have welcomed his story and believed it all,
but now it was too late.

'Samba the Coward,' cried a voice from the crowd; and the
name stuck to him, even the very children shouted it and his
father did not spare him. At length he could bear it no longer
and made up his mind to leave his own land for one where
peace had reigned since the memory of man. So, early next
morning, he slipped out to the king's stables and, choosing
the quietest horse, rode away northward.

Never as long as he lived did Samba forget the terrors of
that journey. He could hardly sleep at night for dread of the
wild beasts that might be lurking behind every rock or bush,
while by day the distant roar of a lion would cause him to
start so violently he almost fell from his horse. A dozen times
he was on the point of turning back, and it was not the terror
of the mocking words and scornful laughs that kept him from
doing so, but the terror lest he should be forced to take part

in their wars. Deeply thankful he felt when the walls of a city, larger than he had ever dreamed of, rose before him.

Drawing himself up to his full height, he rode proudly through the gate and past the palace where, as was her custom, the princess was sitting on the terrace roof, watching the bustle in the street below.

That is a gallant figure, thought she, as Samba, mounted on his big black horse, steered his way skillfully among the crowds. Beckoning to a slave, she ordered him to meet the stranger and ask him who he was and whence he came.

'Oh, Princess, he is the son of a king, and heir to a country which lies near the Great River,' answered the slave, when he had returned from questioning Samba. The princess on hearing this news summoned her father and told him that if she was not allowed to wed the stranger she would die unmarried.

The king could refuse his daughter nothing, and besides, she had rejected so many suitors already he was quite alarmed lest no man should be good enough for her. Therefore, after a talk with Samba, who charmed him by his good humor and pleasant ways, he gave his consent, and three days later the wedding feast was celebrated with the utmost splendor.

The princess was very proud of her tall handsome husband, and for some time she was quite content that he should pass the days with her under the palm trees, telling her stories she loved, or amusing her with tales of the manners and customs of his country. But, by-and-by, this was not enough; she wanted other people to be proud of him too, and one day she said:

'I really almost wish those Moorish thieves from the north would come on one of their expeditions. I should love so to see you ride out at the head of our men to chase them home again. Ah, how happy I should be when the city rang with your noble deeds!'

She looked lovingly at him as she spoke; but to her surprise, his face grew dark, and he answered hastily:

'Never speak to me again of the Moors or of war. It was to escape from them that I fled from my own land, and at the first word of invasion I should leave you forever.'

'How funny you are,' cried she, breaking into a laugh, 'the idea of anyone as big as you being afraid of a Moor! But still, you mustn't say those things to anyone except me, or they might think you were in earnest.'

NOT very long after this, when the people were holding a great feast outside the walls of the town, a body of Moors, who had been in hiding for days, drove off all the sheep and goats which were peacefully feeding on the slopes of a hill. Directly the loss was discovered, the king gave orders that the war drum should be beaten. The warriors assembled in the great square before the palace, trembling with fury at the insult which had been put upon them. Loud were the cries for instant vengeance and for Samba, son-in-law of the king, to lead them to battle. But shout as they might, Samba never came.

Where was he? No farther than in a cool, dark cellar of the palace, crouching among huge earthenware pots of grain. With pain at her heart, there his wife found him, and she tried with all her strength to kindle in him a sense of shame, but in vain. Even the thought of the future danger he might run from the contempt of his subjects was as nothing when compared with the risks of the present.

'Take off your tunic of mail,' said the princess at last. Her voice was so stern and cold that none would have known it. 'Give it to me, and hand me besides your helmet, your sword and your spear.'

And with many fearful glances to right and to left, Samba stripped off the armor inlaid with gold, the property of the king's son-in-law. Silently his wife took the pieces, one by one, and fastened them on herself with firm hands, never even glancing at the tall form of her husband who had slunk back to his corner. When she had fastened the last buckle and lowered her vizor, she went out and, mounting Samba's horse, gave the signal to the warriors to follow.

Now, although the princess was much shorter than her husband, she was a tall woman, and the horse which she rode was likewise higher than the rest, so that when the men caught sight of the gold-inlaid suit of chain armor, they did not doubt that Samba was taking his rightful place and cheered him loudly. The princess bowed in answer to their greeting, but kept her vizor down. Touching her horse with the spur, she galloped at the head of her troops to charge the enemy. The Moors had not expected to be so quickly pursued and were speedily put to flight. Then the little troop of horsemen returned to the city, where all sang the praises of Samba, their leader.

The instant they reached the palace the princess flung her reins to a groom and disappeared up a side staircase, by which she could, unseen, enter her own rooms. Here she found Samba lying idly on a heap of mats; but he raised his head uneasily as the door opened and looked at his wife, not feeling sure how she might act toward him. However, he need not have been afraid of harsh words. She merely unfastened her armor as fast as possible and bade him put it on with all speed. Samba obeyed, not daring to ask any questions. When he had finished, the princess told him to follow her and led him on to the flat roof of the house, below which a crowd had gathered, cheering lustily.

'Samba, the king's son-in-law! Samba, the bravest of the brave! Where is he? Let him show himself!' And when Samba did show himself the shouts and applause became louder than ever. 'See how modest he is! He leaves the glory to others!' cried they. And Samba only smiled and waved his hand, and said nothing.

Out of all the mass of people assembled there to do honor to Samba, one alone did not shout and praise with the rest. This was the princess' youngest brother, whose sharp eyes had noted certain things during the fight which recalled his sister much more than they did her husband. Under promise of secrecy, he told his suspicions to the other princes, but they only laughed and bade him carry his dreams elsewhere.

'Well, well,' answered the boy, 'we shall see who is right. But the next time we give battle to the Moors I will take care to place a private mark on our commander.'

In spite of their defeat, the Moors sent a fresh body of troops to steal some cattle, and again Samba's wife dressed herself in her husband's armor and rode out at the head of the avenging column. This time the combat was fiercer than before, and in the thick of it her youngest brother drew near, and gave his sister a slight wound on the leg. At the moment she paid no heed to the pain which, indeed, she scarcely felt. When the enemy had been put to flight and the little band returned to the palace, faintness suddenly overtook her, and she could hardly stagger to her own apartments.

'I am wounded,' she cried, sinking down on the mats where he had been lying, 'but do not be anxious; it is really nothing. You have only got to wound yourself slightly in the same spot and no one will guess that it was I and not you fighting.'

'What!' cried Samba, his eyes nearly starting from his head in surprise and terror. 'Can you possibly imagine that I should agree to anything so useless and painful? Why, I might as well have gone to fight myself!'

'Ah, I ought to have known better, indeed,' answered the princess, in a voice that seemed to come from a long way off. But quick as thought, the moment Samba turned his back, she pierced one of his bare legs with a spear.

He gave a loud scream and staggered backward, from astonishment much more than from pain. But before he could speak his wife had left the room and had gone to seek the medicine man of the palace.

'My husband has been wounded,' said she. 'Come and tend him with speed, for he is faint from loss of blood.' And she took care that more than one person heard her words, so that all that day the people pressed up to the gate of the palace, asking for news of their brave champion.

'You see,' observed the king's eldest sons, who had visited the room where Samba lay groaning, 'you see, oh, wise young brother, that we were right and you were wrong about Samba,

The princess dealt the horse a sharp cut

and that he really did go into the battle.' But the boy answered nothing and only shook his head doubtfully.

It was only two days later that the Moors appeared for the third time, and though the herds had been tethered in a new and safer place, they were promptly carried off as before. 'For,' said the Moors to each other, 'the tribe will never think of our coming back so soon when they have beaten us so badly.'

When the drum sounded to assemble all the fighting men, the princess rose and sought her husband.

'Samba,' cried she, 'my wound is worse than I thought. I can scarcely walk and could not mount my horse without help. For today, then, I cannot do your work, so you must go instead of me.'

'What nonsense!' exclaimed Samba. 'I never heard of such a thing. Why, I might be wounded or even killed! You have three brothers. The king can choose one of them.'

'They are all too young,' replied his wife. 'The men would not obey them. But if, indeed, you will not go, at least you can help me harness my horse.' And Samba, who was always ready to do anything he was asked when there was no danger about it, agreed readily. So the horse was quickly harnessed, and when it was ready, the princess said:

'Now ride the horse to the place of meeting outside the gates, and I will join you by a shorter way, and will change places with you.' Samba, who loved riding in times of peace, mounted as she bade him, and when he was safe in the saddle, his wife dealt the horse a sharp cut with her whip, and he dashed off through the town and through the ranks of the warriors. Instantly the whole place was in motion. Samba tried to check his steed, but he might as well have sought to stop the wind. It seemed no more than a few minutes before they were grappling hand to hand with the Moors.

Then a miracle happened. Samba the coward, the skulker, the terrified, no sooner found himself pressed hard, unable to escape, than something sprang into life within him and he fought with all his might. And when a man of his size and strength begins to fight he generally fights well.

That day the victory was really owing to Samba, and the shouts of the people were louder than ever. When he returned, bearing with him the sword of the Moorish chief, the old king pressed him in his arms and said:

'Oh, my son, how can I ever show you how grateful I am for this splendid service?'

But Samba, who was good and loyal when fear did not possess him, answered straightly:

'My father, it is to your daughter and not to me to whom thanks are due, for it is she who has turned the coward that I was into a brave man.'

[*Contes Soudainais*, par C. Monteil.]

Diamond Cut Diamond

IN A SMALL VILLAGE IN
Hindustan there once lived a merchant who, although he
rose early, worked hard, and rested late, remained very poor;
and ill luck so dogged him that he determined at last to go
to some distant country and there to try his fortune. Twelve
years passed by; his luck had turned, and now he had gathered
great wealth, so having plenty to keep him in comfort for the
rest of his days, he thought once more of his native village,
where he desired to spend the remainder of his life among
his own people.

In order to carry his riches with him in safety over the many
weary miles that lay between him and his home, he bought
some magnificent jewels, which he locked up in a little box
and wore concealed upon his person. To avoid the attention
of the thieves, who infested the highways and made their living by robbing travelers, he started off in the poor clothes of
a man who has nothing to lose.

Within a few days' journey from his own village he came
to a city where he determined to buy better garments and—
now that he was no longer afraid of thieves—to look more like
the rich man he had become. In his new raiment he approached

the great gate and found a bazaar where, amongst the shops filled with costly silks, carpets and goods of all countries, was one finer than all the rest. There, amidst his goods spread out to the best advantage, sat the owner smoking a long silver pipe, and thither the merchant bent his steps and, saluting him politely, sat down also and began to make some purchases.

Now, the owner of the shop, Beeka Mull by name, was a very shrewd man, and as he and the merchant conversed, he soon felt sure that his customer was richer than he seemed and was trying to conceal the fact. Certain purchases having been made, he invited the newcomer to refresh himself, and in a short time they were chatting pleasantly together. In the course of the conversation Beeka Mull asked the merchant whither he was traveling, and hearing the name of the village, he observed:

'Ah, you had better be careful on that road. It's a very bad place for thieves.'

The merchant turned pale at these words. It would be a bitter thing, he thought, just at the end of his journey to be robbed of all the fortune he had heaped up with such care. But this bland and prosperous Beeka Mull must surely know best, so presently he said:

'Lala-ji, could you oblige me by locking up a small box for a short while? When once I get to my village I could bring back half a dozen sturdy men of my own kinsfolk and claim it again.'

The lala shook his head. 'I could not do it,' replied he. 'I am sorry; but such things are not my business. I should be afraid to undertake it.'

'But,' pleaded the merchant, 'I know no one in this city, and you must surely have some place where you keep your own precious things. Do this, I pray you, as a great favor.'

Still Beeka Mull politely but firmly refused. But the merchant, feeling he had now betrayed the fact that he was richer than he seemed, and being loth to make more people aware of it by inquiring elsewhere, continued to press him, until at last he consented. The merchant produced the little box of jewels, and Beeka Mull locked it up for him in a strong chest with other precious stones. And so, with many promises and compliments, they parted.

In a place like an Eastern bazaar, where the shops lie with wide-open fronts, and with their goods displayed not only within but without on terraces and verandahs raised a few feet above the public roadway, such a long talk as that between Beeka Mull and the merchant could not but attract attention.

If the merchant had but known it, nearly every shopowner in that district was a thief, and the cleverest and biggest of all was Beeka Mull. As he wandered down the street, making a purchase here and there, he managed in one way and another to ask some questions about the honesty of Beeka Mull, and each rascal, hoping to get in return some share of the spoils, replied in praise of Beeka Mull as a model of all the virtues.

In this way the merchant's fears were stilled, and with a comparatively light heart, he traveled on to his village. Within a week or so he returned to the city with half a dozen sturdy young nephews and friends, enlisted to help him carry home his precious box.

At the great market place in the center of the city the merchant left his friends, saying he would go for the box of jewels and rejoin them, to which they consented, and away he went. Arrived at the shop of Beeka Mull, he went up and saluted him.

'Good day, Lala-ji,' said he. But the lala pretended not to see him. So he repeated the salutation.

'What do you want?' snapped Beeka Mull. 'You've said your "good day" twice, why don't you tell me your business?'

'Don't you remember me?' asked the merchant.

'Remember you?' growled the other. 'No, why should I? I have plenty to do to remember good customers without trying to remember every beggar who comes whining for charity.'

When he heard this the merchant began to tremble.

'Lala-ji,' he cried, 'surely you remember me and the little box I gave you to take care of! And you promised—yes, indeed, you promised very kindly—that I might return to claim it, and—'

'You scoundrel,' roared Beeka Mull, 'get out of my shop! Be off with you, you impudent scamp! Everyone knows I never keep treasures for anyone; I have trouble enough to do to keep my own! Come, off with you!'

With that he began to push the merchant out of the shop; and when the poor man resisted, two of the bystanders came to Beeka Mull's help and flung the merchant out into the road, like a bale of goods dropped from a camel. Slowly he picked himself up out of the dust, bruised, battered and bleeding, but feeling nothing of the pain in his body, nothing but a dreadful numbing sensation that, after all, he was ruined and lost! Slowly he dragged himself a little farther from where the fat and furious Beeka Mull still stood amongst his disordered silks and carpets. Coming to a friendly wall the merchant crouched and leaned against it and, putting his head into his hands, gave himself up to an agony of misery and despair.

There he sat motionless, like one turned to stone, while darkness fell around him; and when, about eleven o'clock that night, a certain gay young fellow named Kooshy Ram passed by with a friend, he saw the merchant sitting hunched against the wall, and remarked, 'A thief, no doubt.' 'You are wrong,' returned the other, 'thieves do not sit in full view of people like that, even at night.' And so the two passed on and thought no more of him.

About five o'clock next morning Kooshy Ram was returning home again when, to his astonishment, he saw the miserable merchant still sitting as he had seen him six hours before. Surely something must be the matter with a man who sat all night in the open street. Kooshy Ram resolved to see what it was; so he went up and shook the merchant gently by the shoulder.

'Who are you?' asked he. 'What are you doing here—are you ill?'

'Ill?' said the merchant in a hollow voice. 'Yes; ill with a sickness for which there is no medicine.'

'Oh, nonsense!' cried Kooshy Ram. 'Come along with me, I know a medicine that will cure you, I think.' So the young man seized the merchant by the arm and, hoisting him to his feet, dragged him to his own lodging; where he first of all gave him a large glass of wine, and then, after he had refreshed him with food, bade him tell his adventures.

MEANWHILE the merchant's companions in the market place, being dull-witted persons, thought that as he did not return he must have gone home by himself; and as soon as they were tired of waiting they went back to their village and left him to look after his own affairs. He would therefore have fared badly had it not been for his rescuer. Kooshy Ram, while still a boy, had been left a great deal of money with no one to advise him how to spend it. He was high-spirited, kind-hearted and shrewd into the bargain. Now, he had taken it into his head to befriend this miserable merchant, and he meant to do it. On his side the merchant felt his confidence revive and without further ado told all that had happened.

Kooshy Ram laughed heartily at the idea of any stranger entrusting his wealth to Beeka Mull.

'Why, he is the greatest rascal in the city,' he cried. 'Well, there is nothing to be done for the present, but just to stay here quietly, and I think that at the end of a short time I shall find a medicine to heal your sickness.' At this the merchant again took courage, and a little ease crept into his heart as he gratefully accepted his new friend's invitation.

A few days later Kooshy Ram sent for some friends and talked with them long, and although the merchant did not hear the conversation, he did hear shouts of laughter as though at some good joke. The laughter echoed dully in his own heart, for the more he considered the more he despaired of ever recovering his fortune from the grasp of Beeka Mull.

One day, soon after this, Kooshy Ram came to him and said, 'You remember the wall where I found you that night, near Beeka Mull's shop?'

'Yes, indeed I do,' answered the merchant.

'Well,' continued Kooshy Ram, 'this afternoon you must go and stand in that same spot and watch. When someone gives you a signal, you must go up to Beeka Mull, salute him, and say, "Oh, Lala-ji, will you kindly let me have back that box of mine which you have on trust?" '

'What's the use of that?' asked the merchant. 'He won't do it any more now than he would when I asked him before.'

'Never mind,' replied Kooshy Ram, 'do exactly what I tell you, and repeat exactly what I say, word for word. I will answer for the rest.'

So, that afternoon, the merchant stood by the wall as he was told. Beeka Mull saw him, but neither took any heed of the other. Presently up to the bazaar came a gorgeous palanquin like those in which ladies of rank are carried about. It was borne by four bearers well dressed in rich liveries, and its curtains and trappings were truly magnificent. In attendance was a grave-looking personage whom the merchant recognized as one of the friends who visited Kooshy Ram, and behind him came a servant with a box covered with a cloth upon his head.

The palanquin was borne along at a smart pace and was set down at Beeka Mull's shop. The shopkeeper was on his feet at once and bowed deeply as the gentleman in attendance advanced.

'May I inquire,' he said, 'who this is in the palanquin, who deigns to favor my humble shop with a visit? And what may I do for her?'

The gentleman, after whispering at the curtain of the palanquin, explained that this was a relative of his who was traveling, but as her husband could go no farther with her, she desired to leave with Beeka Mull a box of jewels for safe custody.

The palanquin was set down at Beeka Mull's shop

Lala bowed again to the ground. 'It is not,' he said, 'quite in my way of business; but of course, if I can please the lady, I would be most happy and would guard the box with my life.'

Then the servant carrying the box was called up. The box was unlocked and a mass of jewelery laid open to the gaze of the enraptured Lala, whose mouth watered as he turned over the rich gems.

All this the merchant had watched from the distance, and now he saw—could he be mistaken? No, he distinctly saw a hand beckoning through the curtain on that side of the palanquin away from the shop. The signal! Was this the signal? thought he. The hand beckoned again, impatiently it seemed to him. So forward he went, very quietly, and saluting Beeka Mull, who was turning over the contents of this amazing box of jewels which fortune and some fools were putting into his care, he said:

'O Lala-ji, will you kindly let me have back that box of mine which you have on trust?'

The Lala looked up as though he had been stung. But quickly the thought flashed through his mind that, if this man began making a fuss again, he would lose the confidence of these new and richer customers, so he controlled himself, and answered:

'Dear me, of course, yes! I had forgotten all about it.' And he went off and brought the little box and put it into the merchant's trembling hands. Quickly the latter pulled out the key, which hung by a string round his neck, and opened the box. When he saw that his treasures were all there he rushed into the road and, with the box under his arms, began dancing like a madman, with great shouts and screams of laughter. Just then a messenger came running up and, saluting the gentleman attending the palanquin, he said:

'The lady's husband has returned and is prepared to travel with her so there is no necessity to deposit the jewels.' Whereat the gentleman quickly closed and relocked the box and handed it back to the waiting servant. Then from the palanquin came a yell of laughter, and out jumped—not a lady—but Kooshy Ram, who immediately ran and joined the merchant in the middle of the road and danced as madly as he. Beeka Mull stood and stared stupidly at them. Then, with a shrill cackle of laughter, he flung off his turban, bounced out into the road with the other two, and fell to dancing and snapping his fingers until he was out of breath.

'Lala-ji,' said the gentleman who had played the part of the relative attendant on the palanquin, 'why do you dance? The merchant dances because he has recovered his fortune; Kooshy Ram dances because he is a madman and has tricked you; but why do you dance?'

'I dance,' panted Beeka Mull, glaring at him with bloodshot eyes, 'I dance because I knew thirteen different ways of deceiving people by pretending confidence in them. I didn't know there were any more, and now here's a fourteenth! That's why I dance!'

[Punjâbi story, Major Campbell, Feroshepore.]

The Five Wise Words

ONCE THERE LIVED A handsome young man named Ram Singh who, though a favorite with everyone, was unhappy because he had a scold for a stepmother. All day long she went on talking, until the youth was so distracted he determined to go away and seek his fortune. No sooner had he decided to leave his home than he made his plans, and the very next morning he started off with a few clothes in a wallet and a little money in his pocket.

But there was one person in the village to whom he wished to say good-bye, and that was a wise old guru, or teacher, who had taught him much. So he turned his face first of all toward his master's hut and, before the sun was well up, was knocking at his door.

The old man received his pupil affectionately; but he was wise in reading faces, and saw at once that the youth was in trouble.

'My son,' said he, 'what is the matter?'

'Nothing, father,' replied the young man, 'but I have determined to go into the world and seek my fortune.'

'Be advised,' returned the guru, 'and remain in your father's

house. It is better to have half a loaf at home than to seek a
whole one in distant countries.'

But Ram Singh was in no mood to heed such advice, and
very soon the old man ceased to press him.

'Well,' said he at last, 'if your mind is made up, I suppose
you must have your way. But listen carefully, and remember
five parting counsels which I will give you; if you keep these
no evil shall befall you. First, always obey without question the
orders of him whose service you enter; second, never speak
harshly or unkindly to anyone; third, never lie; fourth, never
try to appear the equal of those above you in station; and
fifth, wherever you go, if you meet those who read or teach
from the holy books, stay and listen, if but for a few minutes,
that you may be strengthened in the path of duty.'

Then Ram Singh started out upon his journey, promising
to bear in mind the old man's words.

After some days he came to a great city. He had spent all
the money he had brought with him, and therefore resolved
to look for work, however humble it might be. Catching sight
of a prosperous-looking merchant standing in front of a grain
shop, Ram Singh asked whether he could give him anything
to do.

The merchant gazed at him so long the young man began
to lose heart, but at length he answered, 'Yes, of course; there
is a place waiting for you.'

'What do you mean?' asked Ram Singh.

'Why,' replied the other, 'yesterday our rajah's chief wazir
dismissed his body servant and is wanting another. Now you
are just the sort of person he needs, for you are young and
tall and handsome. I advise you to apply there.'

Thanking the merchant for this advice, the young man set
out at once for the wazir's house. He soon managed, thanks to

his good looks and appearance, to be engaged as the great man's servant.

One day, soon after this, the rajah of the place started on a journey and the chief wazir accompanied him. With them was an army of servants and attendants, soldiers, muleteers, camel drivers, merchants with grain and stores for man and beast, singers to make entertainment by the way and musicians to accompany them, besides elephants, camels, horses, mules, ponies, donkeys, goats, and carts and wagons of every kind and description. It seemed more like a large town on the march than anything else.

Thus they traveled till they entered a country that was like a sea of sand, where the swirling dust floated in clouds, and men and beasts were half choked by it. Toward the close of day they came to a village. The headmen hurried out to salute the rajah and to pay him their respects, but the people began, with very long and serious faces, to explain that, while they and all they had were of course at the disposal of the rajah, the coming of so large a company had nevertheless put them into a dreadful difficulty. They had neither a well nor spring of water in their country and they had no water to give drink to such an army of men and beasts!

Great fear fell upon the host at the words of the headmen, but the rajah merely told the wazir that he must get water somehow, and that settled the matter so far as he was concerned. The wazir sent off in haste for all the oldest men in the place, and began to question them as to whether there were no wells near by.

They all looked helplessly at each other, and said nothing; but at length one old graybeard replied, 'Truly, Sir Wazir, there is, within a mile or two of this village, a well which some former king made hundreds of years ago. It is, they say, great and inexhaustible, covered in by heavy stonework and with a flight of steps leading down to the water in the very bowels of the earth. But no man ever goes near it because it is haunted by evil spirits, and it is known that whosoever disappears down the well shall never be seen again.'

The wazir stroked his beard and considered a moment. Then he turned to Ram Singh who stood behind his chair.

'There is a proverb,' said he, 'that no man can be trusted until he has been tried. Go you and get the rajah and his people water from this well.'

Then there flashed into Ram Singh's mind the first counsel of the old guru, *Always obey without question the orders of him whose service you enter.* So he replied at once that he was ready and left to prepare for his adventure. Two great brazen vessels he fastened to a mule, two lesser ones he bound upon his shoulders, and thus provided he set out, with the old villager for his guide.

In a short time they came to a spot where some big trees towered above the barren country, while under their shadow lay the dome of an ancient building. This the guide pointed out as the well, but excused himself from going farther as he was an old man and tired, and it was already sunset. So Ram Singh bade him farewell and went on alone with the mule.

Arrived at the trees, Ram Singh tied up his beast, lifted the vessels to his shoulder and, having found the opening of the well, descended a flight of steps into the darkness. The steps were broad white slabs of alabaster which gleamed in the shadows as he went lower and lower. All was very silent. Even the sound of his bare feet upon the pavements seemed to wake an echo in that lonely place, and when one of the vessels which he carried slipped and fell upon the steps it clanged so loudly he jumped at the noise.

Still he went on, until at last he reached a wide pool of sweet water, and there he washed his jars with care before he filled them and began to remount the steps with the lighter vessels, as the big ones were so heavy he could only take up one at a time. Suddenly, something moved above him, and looking up he saw a great giant standing on the stairway! In one hand he held clasped to his heart a dreadful-looking mass of bones, in the other was a lamp which cast long shadows about the walls and made him seem even more terrible than he really was.

'What think you, O mortal,' said the giant, 'of my fair and lovely wife?' And he held the light toward the bones in his arms and looked lovingly at them.

Now this poor giant had had a very beautiful wife, whom he had loved dearly; but, when she died, her husband refused to believe in her death and always carried her about long after she had become nothing but bones. Ram Singh of course did not know of this, but there came to his mind the second wise saying of the guru, which forbade him to speak harshly or inconsiderately to others; so he replied, 'Truly, sir, I am sure you could find nowhere such another.'

'Ah, what eyes you have!' cried the delighted giant. 'You at least can see! I do not know how often I have slain those who insulted her by saying she was but dried bones! You are a fine young man, and I will help you.'

So saying, he laid down the bones with great tenderness, and snatching up the huge brass vessels, carried them up, and replaced them with such ease that it was all done by the time Ram Singh had reached the open air with the smaller ones.

'Now,' said the giant, 'you have pleased me, and you may ask of me one favor. Whatever you wish I will do for you. Perhaps you would like me to show you where lies buried the treasure of dead kings?' he added eagerly.

But Ram Singh shook his head at the mention of buried wealth. 'The favor I would ask,' said he, 'is that you will leave off haunting this well, so men may go in and out to obtain water.'

Perhaps the giant expected some favor more difficult to grant, for his face brightened, and he promised to depart at once. As Ram Singh went off through the gathering darkness with his precious burden of water, he beheld the giant striding away with the bones of his dead wife in his arms.

Great was the wonder and rejoicing in the camp when Ram Singh returned with the water. He said nothing about his adventure with the giant, but merely told the rajah there was nothing to prevent the well being used. And used it was, and nobody ever saw any more of the giant.

The rajah was so pleased with the bearing of Ram Singh that he ordered the wazir to give the young man to him in exchange for one of his own servants. So Ram Singh became the rajah's attendant; and as the days went by the king became more and more delighted with the youth because, mindful of the old guru's third counsel, he was always honest and spoke the truth. He grew in favor rapidly, until at last the rajah made him his treasurer, and thus he reached a high place in the court and had wealth and power in his hands.

Unluckily, the rajah had a brother who was a very bad man. This brother thought that if he could win the young treasurer over to himself he might by this means manage to steal, little by little, any of the king's treasure which he needed. Then, with plenty of money, he could bribe the soldiers and some of the rajah's councilors, head a rebellion, dethrone and kill his brother, and reign himself.

He was too wary, of course, to tell Ram Singh of all these wicked plans, but he began by flattering him whenever he saw him, and at last offered him his daughter in marriage. But Ram Singh remembered the fourth counsel of the old guru—never to try to appear the equal of those above him in station—therefore he respectfully declined the great honor of marrying a princess. Of course the prince, baffled at the very beginning of his enterprise, was furious and determined to work Ram Singh's ruin. Entering the rajah's presence he told him a story about Ram Singh having spoken insulting words of his sovereign and of his daughter.

What it was all about nobody knew, and as it was not true, the wicked prince did not know either. But the rajah grew very angry and red in the face as he listened, and declared that until the treasurer's head was cut off neither he nor the princess nor his brother would eat or drink.

'But,' added he, 'I do not wish anyone to know that this was done by my desire, and anyone who mentions the subject will be severely punished.' And with this the prince was forced to be content.

Then the rajah sent for an officer of his guard, and told him to take some soldiers and ride at once to a tower outside the town, and if anyone should come to inquire when the building was going to be finished, or should ask any other questions about it, the officer must chop his head off and bring it to him. As for the body, that could be buried on the spot. The old officer thought these instructions rather odd, but it was no business of his, so he saluted, and went off to do his master's bidding.

Early in the morning the rajah, who had not slept all night, sent for Ram Singh and bade him go to the new hunting tower, and ask the people there how it was getting on, when it was going to be finished, and to hurry back with the answer! Away went Ram Singh upon his errand but, on the road, as he was passing a little temple on the outskirts of the city, he heard someone inside reading aloud. Remembering the guru's fifth counsel, he stepped inside and sat down to listen for a minute. He did not mean to stay longer, but became so deeply interested in the wisdom of the teacher, that he sat and sat and sat, while the sun rose higher and higher.

In the meantime, the wicked prince, who dared not disobey the rajah's command, was feeling very hungry, and the princess was quietly crying in a corner, waiting for the news of Ram Singh's death so she might eat her breakfast.

Hours passed, and stare as he might from the window, no messenger could be seen. At last the prince could bear it no longer, and hastily disguising himself so no one should recognize him, he jumped on a horse and galloped out to the hunting tower, where the rajah had told him the execution was to take place. But, when he arrived, there was no execution going on. There were only some men engaged in building, and a number of soldiers idly watching them.

He forgot that he had disguised himself and that no one
would know him, so riding up, he cried out, 'Now then, you
men, why are you idling about here instead of finishing what
you came to do? When is it to be done?'

At his words the soldiers looked at the commanding officer,
who was standing a little apart from the rest. Unperceived by
the prince he made a slight sign, a sword flashed in the sun,
and off flew a head on the ground beneath!

As part of the prince's disguise had been a thick beard, the
men did not recognize the dead man as the rajah's brother.
They wrapped the head in a cloth and buried the body as
their commander bade them. When this was ended, the officer
took the cloth and rode off in the direction of the palace.

Meanwhile the rajah came home from his council, and to
his great surprise found neither head nor brother awaiting
him. As time passed, he became uneasy and thought he had
better go himself and see what the matter was. So ordering
his horse, he rode off alone.

Just as the rajah came near the temple where Ram Singh

still sat, the young treasurer, hearing the sound of a horse's hoofs, looked over his shoulder and saw that the rider was the rajah himself! Feeling much ashamed for having forgotten his errand, he jumped up and hurried out to meet his master, who reined up his horse, and seemed very surprised (as indeed he was) to see him. At that moment there arrived the officer of the guard, carrying his parcel. He saluted the rajah gravely and, dismounting, laid the bundle in the road and began to undo the wrappings, while the rajah watched him with wonder and interest.

When the last string was undone, and the head of his brother was displayed to his view, the rajah sprang from his horse and caught the soldier by the arm. As soon as he could speak he questioned the man as to what had occurred, and little by little a dark suspicion grew. Then, telling the soldier he had done well, the rajah drew Ram Singh to one side, and in a few minutes learned from him how, in attending to the guru's counsel, he had delayed to do the king's message.

In the end the rajah found proofs of his dead brother's treachery, and Ram Singh established his innocence and integrity. He continued to serve the rajah for many years with unswerving fidelity, and married a maiden of his own rank in life, with whom he lived happily, dying at last honored and loved by all men. Sons were born to him; and, in time, to them also he taught the five wise sayings of the old guru.

[A Punjâbi story.]

The Golden-Headed Fish

ONCE UPON A TIME
there lived in Egypt a king who lost his sight from a bad illness. Of course he was very unhappy, and became more so as months passed, and all the best doctors in the land were unable to cure him. The poor man grew so thin from misery that everyone thought he was going to die, and the prince, his only son, thought so too.

Great, therefore, was the rejoicing throughout Egypt when a traveler down the river Nile declared he was court physician to the king of a far country, and would, if allowed, examine the eyes of the blind man. He was 'at once admitted into the royal presence, and after a few minutes of careful study announced that the case, though very serious, was not quite hopeless.

'Somewhere in the Great Sea,' he said, 'there exists a Golden-headed Fish. If you can manage to catch this creature and bring it to me, I will prepare an ointment from its blood which will restore your sight. For a hundred days I will wait here, but if at the end of that time the fish should still be uncaught, I must return to my own master.'

The next morning the young prince set forth in quest of

the fish, taking with him a hundred men, each carrying a net. A little fleet of boats was awaiting them and in these they sailed to the middle of the Great Sea. During three months and more, they labored diligently from sunrise to sunset, but though they caught large multitudes of fishes, not one of them had a golden head.

'It is quite useless now,' said the prince on the very last night. 'Even if we find it this evening, the hundred days will be over in an hour, and long before we could reach the Egyptian capital the doctor will be on his way home. Still, I will go out again and cast the net once more myself.' And so he did, and at the very moment that the hundred days were up, he drew in the net with the Golden-headed Fish entangled in its meshes.

'Success has come, but as happens often, it is too late,' murmured the young man, who had studied in the schools of philosophy. 'But all the same, put the fish in that vessel full of water, and we will take it back to show my father that we have done what we could.' But when he drew near the fish, it looked up at him with such piteous eyes he could not make

up his mind to condemn it to death. For he knew well that, though the doctors of his own country were ignorant of the secret of the ointment, they would do all in their power to extract something from the fish's blood.

So he picked up the prize of so much labor and threw it back into the sea and then began his journey back to the palace. When at last he reached it he found the king in a high fever, caused by his disappointment, and he refused to believe the story told him by his son.

'Your head shall pay for it! Your head shall pay for it!' cried he, and bade the courtiers instantly summon the executioner to the palace.

But of course somebody ran at once to the queen and told her of the king's order. She put common clothes on the prince, filled his pockets with gold, and hurried him on board a ship which was sailing that night for a distant island.

'Your father will repent some day, and then he will be thankful to know you are alive,' said she. 'But one last counsel will I give you; take no man into your service who desires to be paid every month.'

The young prince thought this advice rather odd. If the servant had to be paid anyhow, he did not understand what difference it could make whether it was by the year or by the month. However, he had many times proved that his mother was wiser than he, so he promised obedience.

AFTER a voyage of several weeks, the prince arrived at the island of which his mother had spoken. It was full of hills and woods and flowers, and beautiful white houses stood everywhere in gardens. What a charming spot to live in, thought the prince. And he lost no time in buying one of the prettiest of the dwellings.

Then servants came pressing to offer their services; but as they all declared they must have payment at the end of every month, the young man declined to have anything to say to them. At length, one morning, an Arab appeared and begged the prince to engage him.

'And what wages do you ask?' inquired the prince, when he had questioned the newcomer and found him suitable.

'I do not want money,' answered the Arab. 'At the end of a year you can see what my services are worth to you and can pay me in any way you like.' The young man was pleased and took the Arab for his servant.

Now, although no one would have guessed it from the look of the side of the island where the prince had landed, the other part was a complete desert, owing to the ravages of a horrible monster which came up from the sea and devoured all the corn and cattle. The governor had sent bands of soldiers to lie in wait for the creature in order to kill it, but, somehow, no one ever happened to be awake at the moment the ravages were committed. It was in vain that the sleepy soldiers were punished severely—the same thing invariably occurred next time. At last heralds were sent throughout the island to offer a great reward to the man who could slay the monster.

As soon as the Arab heard the news, he went straight to the governor's palace. 'If my master can succeed in killing the monster, what reward will you give him?' asked he.

'My daughter and anything besides that he chooses,' answered the governor.

But the Arab shook his head.

'Give him your daughter and keep your wealth,' said he. 'But, henceforward, let her share in your gains, whatever they are.'

'It is well,' replied the governor, and ordered a deed to be prepared, which was signed by both of them.

That night the Arab stole down to the shore to watch, but before he set out, he rubbed himself all over with some oil which made his skin smart so badly that there was no chance of his going to sleep as the soldiers had done. Then he hid himself behind a large rock and waited. By-and-by a swell seemed to rise on the water and, a few minutes later, a hideous monster—part bird, part beast and part serpent—stepped noiselessly on to the rocks. It walked stealthily up toward the fields, but the Arab was ready for it and, as it passed, plunged his dagger into the soft part behind the ear. The creature staggered and gave a loud cry, and then rolled over dead, with its feet in the sea.

The Arab watched for a little while, in order to make sure there was no life left in his enemy. As the huge body remained quite still, he quitted his hiding place and cut off its ears. These he carried to his master, bidding him show them to the governor and declare that he himself, and no other, had killed the monster.

'But it was you, and not I, who slew him,' objected the prince.

'Never mind; do as I bid you. I have a reason for it,' answered the Arab. And though the young man did not like taking credit for what he had not done, at length he gave in.

The governor was so delighted at the news that he begged the prince to take his daughter to wife that very day; but the prince refused, saying that all he desired was a ship which would carry him to see the world. Of course this was granted him at once, and when he and his faithful Arab embarked they found, heaped up in the vessel, stores of diamonds and precious stones, which the grateful governor had placed there for him.

So they sailed and they sailed and they sailed, and at length

A hideous monster stepped noiselessly on to the rocks

they reached the shores of a great kingdom. Leaving the prince on board, the Arab went into the town to find out what sort of place it was. After some hours he returned, saying he heard that the king's daughter was the most beautiful princess in the world and the prince would do well to ask for her hand.

Nothing loth, the prince listened to this advice. Taking some of the finest necklaces in his hand, he mounted a splendid horse, which the Arab had bought for him, and rode up to the palace, closely followed by his faithful attendant.

The strange king happened to be in a good humor, and they were readily admitted to his presence. Laying down his offerings on the steps of the throne, the prince prayed the king to grant him his daughter in marriage.

The monarch listened to him in silence; but answered, after a pause, 'Young man, I will give you my daughter to wife, if that is your wish; but first I must tell you that she has already gone through the marriage ceremony with a hundred and ninety young men, and not one of them lived for twelve hours after. So think, while there is yet time.'

The prince did think and was so frightened he very nearly went back to his ship without any more words. But just as he was about to withdraw his proposal the Arab whispered:

'Fear nothing, but take her.'

'The luck must change some time,' he said, at last, 'and who would not risk his head for the hand of such a peerless princess?'

'As you will,' replied the king. 'Then I will give orders for the marriage to be celebrated tonight.'

And so it was done. After the ceremony the bride and bride-groom retired to their own apartments to sup by themselves, for such was the custom of the country. The moon shone bright, and the prince walked to the window to look out upon the river and upon the distant hills, when his gaze suddenly fell on a silken shroud neatly laid out on a couch, with his name embroidered in gold thread across the front; for this also was the pleasure of the king.

Horrified at the spectacle, he turned his head away, and this time his glance rested on a group of men, digging busily beneath the window. It was a strange hour for anyone to be at work, and what was the hole for? It was a curious shape, so long and narrow, almost like— Ah, yes, that was what it was! It was his grave they were digging!

The shock of the discovery rendered him speechless, yet he stood fascinated and unable to move. At this moment a small black snake darted from the mouth of the princess, who was seated at the table, and wriggled quickly toward him. But the Arab was watching for something of the sort to happen and, seizing the serpent with some pincers he held in one hand, he cut off its head with a sharp dagger.

The king could hardly believe his eyes when, early the next morning, his new son-in-law craved an audience of his majesty.

'What, you?' he cried, as the young man entered.

'Yes, I. Why not?' asked the bridegroom, who thought it best to pretend not to know anything that had occurred. 'You remember, I told you that the luck must turn at last, and so it has. But I came to ask whether you would be so kind as to bid the gardeners fill up a great hole right underneath my window; it spoils the view.'

'Oh, certainly. Yes, of course it shall be done!' stammered the king. 'Is there anything else?'

'No, nothing, thank you,' replied the prince, as he bowed and withdrew.

Now, from the moment the Arab cut off the snake's head, the spell, or whatever it was, seemed to have been taken off the princess, and she lived very happily with her husband. The days passed swiftly in hunting in the forests, or sailing on the broad river that flowed past the palace, and when night fell she would sing to her harp, or the prince would tell her tales of his own country.

One evening, a man in a strange garb, with a face burned brown by the sun, arrived at court. He asked to see the bridegroom and, falling on his face, announced that he was a messenger sent by the Queen of Egypt, proclaiming him king in succession to his father, who was dead.

'Her majesty begs you will set out without delay, and your bride also, as the affairs of the kingdom are somewhat in disorder,' ended the messenger.

Then the young man hastened to seek an audience of his father-in-law, who was delighted to find that his daughter's husband was not merely the governor of a province, as he had supposed, but the king of a powerful country. He at once ordered a splendid ship to be made ready, and in a week's time rode down to the harbor, to bid farewell to the young couple.

In spite of her grief for the dead king, the queen was overjoyed to welcome her son home, and commanded the palace to be hung with splendid stuffs to do honor to the bride. The people expected great things from their new sovereign, for they had suffered much from the harsh rule of the old one, and crowds presented themselves every morning with petitions in their hands, which they hoped to persuade the king to grant. Truly, he had enough to keep him busy; but he was very happy for all that, till one night the Arab came to him and begged permission to return to his own land.

Filled with dismay the young man said, 'Leave me! Do you really wish to leave me?'

Sadly the Arab bowed his head. 'No, my master; never

could I wish to leave you! But I have received a summons, and I dare not disobey it.'

The king was silent, trying to choke down the grief he felt at the thought of losing his faithful servant.

'Well, I must not try to keep you,' he faltered at last. 'That would be a poor return for all that you have done for me! Everything I have is yours; take what you will, for without you I should long ago have been dead!'

'And without you, I should long ago have been dead,' answered the Arab. 'I am the Golden-headed Fish.'

[Adapted from *Contes Arméniens,* par Frédéric Macler, Paris. Ernest Leroux, Editeur.]

Dorani

Once upon a time
there lived in a city of Hindustan a seller of scents and essences,
who had a very beautiful daughter named Dorani. This maiden
had a friend who was a fairy, and the two were high in favor
with Indra, the King of Fairyland, because they were able to
sing so sweetly and dance so deftly that no one in the kingdom
could equal them for grace and beauty.

Dorani had the most lovely hair in the world, for it was like
spun gold, and the smell of it was like fresh roses. But her
locks were so long and thick that the weight was often un-
bearable, and one day she cut off a shining tress. Wrapping
it in a large leaf she threw it into the river which ran just
below her window.

Now it happened that the king's son was out hunting and
had gone down to the river to drink, when there floated toward
him a folded leaf, from which came a perfume of roses. The
prince, with idle curiosity, took a step into the water and
caught the leaf as it was sailing by. He opened it, and within
he found a lock of hair like spun gold, from which came a
faint, exquisite odor.

When the prince reached home that day he looked so sad

and was so quiet that his father wondered if any ill had befallen him, and asked what was the matter. Then the youth
took from his breast the tress of hair which he had found in
the river, and holding it up to the light, replied:

'See, my father, was ever hair like this? Unless I may win
and marry the maiden who owns that lock I must die!'

So the king immediately sent heralds throughout all his
dominions to search for the damsel with hair like spun gold,
and at last he learned that she was the daughter of the scentseller. The herald's mission was quickly noised abroad. Dorani
heard of it with the rest, and she said to her father:

'If the hair is mine, and the king requires me to marry his
son, I must do so, but remember, you must tell him that, after
the wedding, if I stay all day at the palace, every night I will
spend in my old home.'

The old man listened to her with amazement, but answered
nothing, for he knew she was wiser than he. Of course the
hair was Dorani's, and heralds soon returned and informed
the king, their master. He summoned the scentseller, and told
him he wished his daughter to be given in marriage to the
prince. The father bowed his head three times to the ground,
and replied:

'Your Highness is our lord, and all that you bid us we will
do. The maiden asks this only—that if, after the wedding, she
stays all day at the palace, she may go back each night to her
father's house.'

The king thought this a very strange request, but said to
himself it was, after all, his son's affair, and the girl would
surely soon get tired of going to and fro. So he made no difficulty. Everything was speedily arranged and the wedding was
celebrated with great rejoicings.

At first, the condition attached to his wedding the lovely

Dorani troubled the prince very little, for he thought he would at least see his bride all day. But to his dismay, he found she would do nothing but sit the whole time upon a stool with her head bowed forward upon her knees. He could never persuade her to say a single word. Each evening she was carried in a palanquin to her father's house, and each morning she was brought back soon after daybreak. Yet never a sound passed her lips, nor did she show by any sign that she saw, or heard, or heeded her husband.

One evening the prince, very unhappy and troubled, was wandering in an old and beautiful garden near the palace. The gardener was a very aged man, who had served the prince's great-grandfather, and when he saw the prince he came and bowed himself before him, and said:

'Child! Child! Why do you look so sad—is aught the matter?'

Then the prince replied, 'I am sad, old friend, because I have married a wife as lovely as the stars, but she will not speak to me, and I know not what to do. Night after night she leaves me for her father's house, day after day she sits in mine

as though turned to stone. She utters no word, whatever I may
do or say.'

The old man stood thinking for a moment, and then he
hobbled off to his own cottage. A little later he came back
to the prince with five or six small packets, which he placed
in his hands, saying:

'Tomorrow, when your bride leaves the palace, sprinkle the
powder from one of these packets upon your body, and while
seeing clearly, you yourself will become invisible. More I cannot do for you, but may all go well!'

The prince thanked him and put the packets carefully away
in his turban.

The next night, when Dorani left for her father's house in
her palanquin, the prince took out a packet of the magic
powder, sprinkled it over himself, and then hurried after her.
He soon found that, as the old man had promised, he was invisible to everyone, although he could see all that passed. He
speedily overtook the palanquin and walked beside it to the
scentseller's dwelling. There it was set down, and when his
bride, closely veiled, left it and entered the house, he, too,
entered unperceived.

At the first door Dorani removed one veil; then she entered
another doorway at the end of a passage where she removed
another veil; next she mounted the stairs, and at the door of
the women's quarters removed a third veil. After this she
proceeded to her own room where were set two large basins,
one of attar of roses and one of water; in these she washed
herself, and afterward called for food. A servant brought her
a bowl of curds, which she ate hastily, and then arrayed herself
in a robe of silver and wound about her strings of pearls, while
a wreath of roses crowned her hair. When fully dressed, she
seated herself upon a four-legged stool over which was a canopy

with silken curtains. She drew them around her, and then called out:

'Fly, stool, to the palace of Rajah Indra.'

Instantly the stool rose in the air, and the invisible prince, who had watched all these proceedings with great wonder, seized it by one leg as it flew away, and found himself being borne along at a rapid rate.

In a short while they arrived at the house of the fairy who was the favorite friend of Dorani. The fairy stood waiting on the threshold, as beautifully dressed as Dorani herself, and when the stool stopped at her door she cried in astonishment:

'Why, the stool is flying all crooked tonight! What is the reason for that, I wonder? I suspect you have been talking to your husband, and so it will not go straight.'

But Dorani declared she had not spoken one word to him, and she couldn't think why the stool flew as if weighed down at one side. The fairy still looked doubtful, but made no answer, and took her seat beside Dorani. Then the stool flew on through the air, the prince again holding tightly to one leg, until it came to the palace of Indra.

All through the night the women sang and danced before Indra, while a magic lute played of itself the most bewitching music. The prince, who sat watching it all, was quite entranced. Just before dawn Indra gave the signal to cease, and again the two women seated themselves on the stool, and with the prince clinging to the leg, it flew back to earth. When Dorani and her husband alighted safely before the scentseller's shop, the prince hurried past the palanquin with its sleepy bearers, straight on to the palace. As he passed the threshold of his own rooms he became visible again. Then he lay down upon a couch and waited for Dorani.

As soon as she arrived she took a seat, silent as usual, with

Dorani danced in the rajah's palace

her head bowed on her knees. For a while not a sound was heard, but presently the prince said:

'I dreamed a curious dream last night. It was all about you and I am going to tell it although you heed nothing.'

The girl did not seem to hear his words, but in spite of that he related every single thing that had happened the evening before, leaving out no detail of all that he had seen or heard. When he praised her singing—and his voice shook a little— Dorani just looked at him. She said naught; though, in her own mind, she was filled with wonder. What a dream! she thought. Could it have been a dream? How could he have learned in a dream all she had done or said? Still she kept silent. She looked only that once at the prince, and then she remained all day as before, with her head bowed upon her knees.

When night came the prince again made himself invisible and followed her. The same things happened again, as had happened before, but Dorani sang better than ever. In the morning the prince a second time told Dorani all she had done, pretending he had dreamed of it. Directly he had finished, Dorani gazed at him, and said:

'Is it true that you dreamed this, or were you really there?'

'I was there,' answered the prince.

'But why do you follow me?' asked the girl.

'Because,' replied the prince, 'I love you, and to be with you is happiness.'

This time Dorani's eyelids quivered, but she said no more, and was silent the rest of the day. However, in the evening, just as she was stepping into her palanquin, she said to the prince:

'If you love me, prove it by not following me tonight.'

The prince did as she wished and stayed at home. That

evening the magic stool flew so unsteadily they could hardly keep their seats, and at last the fairy exclaimed:

'There is only one reason it should jerk like this! You have been talking to your husband!'

And Dorani replied, 'Yes, I have spoken. Oh, yes, I have spoken!' But no more would she say.

That night Dorani sang so marvelously that at the end Indra rose up and vowed she might ask what she would and he would give it to her.

At first she was silent, but when he pressed her, she answered, 'Give me the magic lute.'

The rajah was displeased with himself for having made so rash a promise, because he valued this lute above all his possessions. But as he had promised, so he must perform, and with an ill grace he handed it to her.

'You must never come here again,' said he, 'for once having asked so much, how will you in future be content with smaller gifts?'

Dorani bowed her head silently as she took the lute, and passed with the fairy out of the great gate, where the stool awaited them. More unsteadily than before, it flew back to earth.

When Dorani arrived at the palace that morning she asked the prince whether he had dreamed again. He laughed with happiness, for this time she had spoken to him of her own free will, and he replied:

'No; but I begin to dream now—not of what has happened in the past, but of what may happen in the future.'

That day Dorani sat very quietly, but she answered the prince when he spoke to her. When evening fell, and with it the time for her departure, she still stayed on. Then the prince came close to her and said softly:

'Are you not going to your house, Dorani?'

At that she rose and threw herself weeping into his arms, whispering gently, 'Never again, my lord, never again would I leave you.'

So the prince won his beautiful bride; and though they neither of them dealt any further with fairies and their magic, they learned more daily of the magic of love, which one may still learn, although fairy magic has fled away.

[Punjâbi Story, Major Campbell, Feroshepore.]

The Billy Goat and the King

ONCE THERE LIVED A certain king who understood the language of all birds and beasts and insects. This knowledge had of course been given him by a fairy godmother. It was rather a troublesome present, for he knew that if he were ever to reveal anything he had thus learned he would turn into a stone. How he managed before this story opens I cannot say, but he had safely grown up to manhood, married a wife, and was as happy as monarchs generally are.

Well, one day the king was eating his dinner and his wife was sitting opposite to wait upon him and keep him company. As he ate he dropped some grains of rice upon the ground, and a little ant, who was running about seeking a living, seized upon one of the grains and bore it off toward his hole. Just outside the king's circle this ant met another ant, and the king heard the second one say:

'Oh, dear friend, do give me that grain of rice, and get another one for yourself. You see my boots are so dirty that, if

I were to go upon the king's eating place, I should defile it. I can't do that, it would be so very rude.'

But the owner of the grain of rice only replied, 'If you want rice go and get it. No one will notice your dirty boots. You don't suppose that I am going to carry rice for all our kindred?'

Then the king laughed.

The queen looked at herself up and down, but she could not see or feel anything in her appearance to make the king laugh, so she said, 'What are you laughing at?'

'Did I laugh?' replied the king.

'Of course you did,' retorted the queen. 'And if you think I am ridiculous I wish you would say so, instead of behaving in that stupid way! What are you laughing at?'

'I'm not laughing at anything,' answered the king.

'Very well, but you did laugh, and I want to know why.'

'Well, I'm afraid I can't tell you,' said the king.

'You must tell me,' replied the queen impatiently. 'If you laugh when there's nothing to laugh at you must be ill or mad. What is the matter?'

Still the king refused to say, and still the queen declared she must and would know. For days the quarrel went on and the queen gave her husband no rest, until at last the poor man was almost out of his wits and thought that, as life had become for him hardly worth living while this went on, he might as well tell her the secret and take the consequences.

'But,' he said to himself, 'if I am to become a stone, I am not going to lie, if I can help it, on some dusty highway, to be kicked here and there by man and beast, flung at dogs, be used as the plaything of naughty children, and become generally restless and miserable. I will be a stone at the bottom of the cool river, and roll gently about there until I find some secure resting place where I can stay forever.'

They dismounted in the shade to rest

So he told his wife that if she would ride with him to the middle of the river he would tell her what he had laughed at. She thought he was joking and laughingly agreed; their horses were ordered and they set out.

On the way they came to a fine well beneath the shade of some lofty, wide-spreading trees, and the king proposed they should rest a little, drink some of the cool water, and then pass on. To this the queen consented; so they dismounted in the shade by the well to rest.

It happened that an old goat and his wife were browsing in the neighborhood, and as the king and queen sat there, the nanny goat came to the well's brink and peering over saw some lovely green leaves that sprang in tender shoots out of the side of the well.

'Oh,' cried she to her husband, 'come quickly and look. Here are some leaves which make my mouth water; come and get them for me!'

Then the billy goat sauntered up and looked over, and after that he eyed his wife a little crossly.

'You expect me to get you those leaves, do you? I suppose you don't consider how in the world I am to reach them? You don't seem to think at all; if you did you would know that if I tried to reach those leaves I should fall into the well and be drowned!'

'Oh,' cried the nanny goat, 'why should you fall in? Do try and get them!'

'I am not going to be so silly,' replied the billy goat.

But the nanny goat wept and entreated.

'Look here,' said the billy goat, 'there are plenty of fools in the world, but I am not one of them. This silly king here, because he can't cure his wife of asking questions, is going to throw his life away. But I know how to cure you of your follies and I'm going to.'

And with that he butted the nanny goat so severely that in two minutes she was submissively feeding somewhere else and had made up her mind that the leaves in the well were not worth having.

Then the king, who had understood every word, laughed once more. The queen looked at him suspiciously, but the king got up and walked across to where she sat.

'Are you still determined to find out why I was laughing the other day?' he asked.

'Quite,' answered the queen angrily.

'Because,' said the king, tapping his leg with his riding whip, 'I have made up my mind not to tell you, and moreover, I have made up my mind to stop you mentioning the subject any more.'

'What do you mean?' asked the queen nervously.

'Well,' replied the king, 'I notice that if that goat is displeased with his wife, he just butts her, and that seems to settle the question—'

'Do you mean to say you would beat me?' cried the queen.

'I should be extremely sorry to have to do so,' replied the king; 'but I have to persuade you to go home quietly and to ask no more silly questions when I say I cannot answer them. Of course, if you will persist, why—'

The queen went home, and so did the king. And it is said they are both happier and wiser than ever before.

[Punjâbi Story, Major Campbell, Feroshepore.]

Grasp All, Lose All

ONCE, IN FORMER times, there lived in a certain city in India a poor oilseller, called Déna, who never could keep any money in his pockets. When this story begins he had borrowed from a banker, of the name of Léna, the sum of one hundred rupees, which, with the interest Léna always charged, amounted to a debt of three hundred rupees. Now Déna's business was in a bad way, and he had no money with which to pay his debt. Léna was very angry and used to come round to Déna's house every evening and abuse him until the poor man was nearly worried out of his life.

Léna generally made his visit just when Déna's wife was cooking the evening meal, and would make such a scene that the poor oilseller and his wife and daughter quite lost their appetites and could eat nothing. This went on for some weeks till, one day, Déna said to himself he could stand it no longer and he had better run away. As a man cannot fly easily with a wife and daughter, he thought he must leave them behind. So instead of turning into his house as usual after his day's work, he just slipped out of the city without knowing very well where he was going.

At about ten o'clock that night Déna came to a well by the wayside, near which grew a giant peepul tree. As he was very tired, he determined to climb it and rest for a little before continuing his journey in the morning. Up he went and curled himself so comfortably amongst the great branches that, overcome with weariness, he fell fast asleep.

While he slept some spirits, who roam about such places on certain nights, picked up the tree and flew away with it to a faraway shore where no creature lived, and there, long before the sun rose, they set it down. Just then the oilseller awoke, but instead of finding himself in the midst of a forest, he was amazed to behold nothing but waste shore and wide sea and was dumb with horror and astonishment.

He sat up, trying to collect his senses, and began to catch sight here and there of twinkling, flashing lights, like little fires, that moved and sparkled all about, and he wondered what they were. Presently he saw one so close to him that he reached out his hand and grasped it, and found that it was a sparkling red stone, scarcely smaller than a walnut. He opened a corner of his loincloth and tied the stone in it; and by-and-by he caught another, then a third and a fourth, all of which he tied up carefully in his cloth. At last, just as the day was breaking, the tree rose and, flying rapidly through the air, was deposited once more by the well where it had stood the previous evening.

When Déna had recovered a little from the fright which the extraordinary antics of the tree had caused him, he began to thank Providence he was alive, and as his love of wandering had been quite cured, he made his way back to the city and to his own house. Here he was met and soundly scolded by his wife, who assailed him with a hundred questions and reproaches. As soon as she paused for breath, Déna replied:

'I have only this one thing to say, just look what I have brought!' And, after carefully shutting all the doors, he opened the corner of his loincloth and showed her the four stones, which glittered and flashed as he turned them over and over.

'Pooh,' said his wife, 'the silly pebbles! If it was something to eat, now, there'd be some sense in them; but what's the good of such things?' She turned away with a sniff, for it had happened that the night before, when Léna had come round as usual to storm at Déna, he had been rather disturbed to find his victim was from home and had frightened the poor woman by his threats. Directly, however, he heard that Déna had come back, Léna appeared in the doorway. For some minutes he talked to the oilseller at the top of his voice, until he was tired; then Déna said:

'If your honor would deign to walk into my humble dwelling, I will speak.'

So Léna walked in, and Déna, shutting all the doors, untied the corner of his loincloth and showed him the four great flashing stones.

'This is all,' said he, 'that I have in the world to set against my debt, for, as your honor knows, I haven't a penny, but the stones are pretty!'

Now Léna saw at once that these were magnificent rubies, and his mouth watered for them. But as it would never do to show what was in his mind, he went on:

'What do I care about your stupid stones? It is my money I want, my lawful debt which you owe me, and I shall get it out of you yet, somehow or other, or it will be the worse for you.'

To all his reproaches Déna could answer nothing, but sat with his hands joined together beseechingly, asking for pa-

tience and pity. At length Léna pretended that, rather than
have a bad debt on his hand, he would be at the loss of taking
the stones in lieu of his money; and, while Déna nearly wept
with gratitude, he wrote out a receipt for the three hundred
rupees. Wrapping the four stones in a cloth, he put them into
his bosom, and went off to his house.

'How shall I turn these rubies into money?' said Léna to
himself, as he walked along. 'I daren't keep them, for they are
of great value, and if the rajah heard I had them he would probably put me into prison on some pretence and seize the stones
and all else that I have as well. But what a bargain I have!
Four rubies worth a king's ransom for one hundred rupees!
Well, well, I must take heed not to betray my secret.' And he
went on making plans. Presently he made up his mind what
to do, and, putting on his cleanest clothes, he set off to the
house of the chief wazir, whose name was Musli, and after
seeking a private audience, he brought out the four rubies and
laid them before him.

The wazir's eyes sparkled as he beheld the splendid gems.
'Fine, indeed,' murmured he. 'I can't buy them at their real
value, but if you like to take it, I will give you ten thousand
rupees for the four.'

To this the banker consented gratefully, and handing over
the stones in exchange for the rupees, he hurried home, thanking his stars he had driven such a reasonable bargain and
obtained such an enormous profit.

After Léna had departed, the wazir began casting about in
his mind what to do with the gems, and very soon he determined that the best thing to do was to present them to Rajah
Kahré. Without losing a moment, he went that very day to
the palace and sought a private interview with the rajah. When

he found himself alone with his royal master, he laid the four jewels before him.

'Oh, ho!' said the rajah. 'These are priceless gems, and you have done well to give them to me. In return I will give you and your heirs the revenues of ten villages.'

Now the wazir was overjoyed at these words but only made his deepest obeisance, and while the rajah put the rubies into his turban, he hurried away, beaming with happiness at the thought that for ten thousand rupees he had become lord of ten villages. The rajah was also equally pleased, and strolled off with his new purchases to the women's quarters. He showed them to the rani who was nearly out of her mind with delight. Then, as she turned them over and over in her hands, she said, 'Ah, if I had eight more such gems, what a necklace they would make! Get me eight more of them or I shall die!'

'Most unreasonable of women,' cried the rajah, 'where am I to get eight more such jewels as these? I gave ten villages for them, and yet you are not satisfied!'

'What does it matter?' asked the rani. 'Do you want me to die? Surely you can get some more where these came from?' Then she fell to weeping and wailing until the rajah promised that in the morning he would make arrangements to get some more such rubies, and that if she would be patient she should have her desire.

In the morning the rajah sent for the wazir and said he must manage to get eight more rubies like those he had brought him the day before. 'And if you don't I shall hang you,' cried the rajah, for he was very cross. The poor wazir protested in vain that he knew not where to seek them; his master would not listen to a word he said.

'You must,' said he; 'the rani shall not die for the want of a few rubies! Get more where those came from.'

THE wazir left the palace, much troubled in mind, and bade his slaves bring Léna before him. 'Get me eight more such rubies as those you brought yesterday,' commanded the wazir, directly the banker was shown into his presence. 'Eight more, and be quick, or I am a dead man.'

'But how can I?' wailed Léna. 'Rubies like those do not grow upon bushes!'

'Where did you get them from?' asked the wazir.

'From Déna, the oilseller,' said the banker.

'Well, send for him and ask him where he got them,' answered the wazir. 'I am not going to hang for twenty Dénas!' And more slaves were sent to summon the oilseller.

When Déna arrived he was closely questioned, and then all three started to see the rajah, and to him Déna told the whole story.

'What night was it that you slept in the peepul tree?' demanded the rajah.

'I can't remember,' said Déna. 'But my wife will know.'

Then Déna's wife was sent for, and she explained that it was on the last Sunday of the new moon.

Now everyone knows that it is on the Sunday of the new moon that spirits have special power to play pranks upon mortals. So the rajah forbade them all, on pain of death, to say a word to anyone, and declared that, on the next Sunday of the new moon, they four—Kahré, Musli, Léna and Déna—would go and sit in the peepul tree and see what happened.

The days dragged on to the appointed Sunday, and that evening the four met secretly and entered the forest. They had not far to go before they reached the peepul tree, into which they climbed as the rajah had planned. At midnight the tree began to sway, and presently it moved through the air.

'See, sire,' whispered Déna, 'the tree is flying!'

'Yes, yes,' said the rajah, 'you have told the truth. Now sit quiet, and we shall see what happens.'

Away and away flew the tree with the four men clinging tightly to its branches, until at last it was set down by the waste seashore where a great wide sea came tumbling in on a desert beach. Presently, as before, they began to see little points of light that glistened like fires all around them. Then Déna said to himself:

'Think, last time I only took four that came close to me and I got rid of all my debt in return. This time I will take all I can get and be rich!'

'If I got ten thousand rupees for four stones,' said Léna, 'I will gather forty now for myself and become so wealthy they will probably make me a wazir at least!'

'For four stones I received ten villages,' Musli was silently saying; 'now I will get stones enough to purchase a kingdom, become a rajah, and employ wazirs of my own!'

And Kahré said, 'What is the good of getting only eight stones? Why, here are enough to make twenty necklaces; and wealth means power!'

Full of avarice and desire, each scrambled down from the tree, spread his cloth, and darted hither and thither, picking up the precious jewels, looking the while over his shoulder to see whether his neighbor fared better than he. So engrossed were they in the business of gathering wealth that the dawn came upon them unawares; and suddenly the tree rose up again and flew away, leaving them upon the seashore staring after it, each with his cloth heavy with priceless jewels.

MORNING broke in the city, and great was the consternation in the palace when the chamberlains declared that the rajah had gone out the evening before and had not returned.

Away and away flew the tree

'Ah,' said one, 'it is all right! Musli will know where he is, for he was the king's companion.'

Then they went to the wazir's house, and there they learned that the wazir had left it the evening before and had not returned. 'But,' said a servant, 'Léna the banker will know where he is, for Musli went with him!'

Then they visited the house of Léna, only to learn that the banker had gone out the evening before, and that he too had not returned. But the porter told them that he was accompanied by Déna the oilseller, so he would know where they were.

So they departed to Déna's house, and Déna's wife met them with a torrent of reproaches and wailings, for Déna too had gone off the evening before to Léna's house and had not returned.

In vain they waited and searched—never did any of the hapless four return to their homes; and the confused tale which was told by Déna's wife was the only clue to their fate. To this day, in that country, when a greedy man has overreached himself, and lost all in grasping at too much, folks say:

'All has he lost! Neither Déna nor Léna nor Musli nor Kahré remain.' And not five men in a hundred know how the proverb began, nor what it really signifies.

[Major Campbell, Feroshepore.]

The Fate of the Turtle

IN A VERY HOT COUN-
try, far away to the east, was a beautiful little lake where two
wild ducks made their home, and passed their days swimming
and playing in its clear waters. They had it all to themselves,
except for a turtle, who was many years older than they were,
and had come there before them and, luckily, instead of taking
a dislike to the turtle, as so often happens when you have only
one person to speak to, they became great friends, and spent
most of the day in each other's company.

All went on smoothly and happily till one summer, when
the rains failed and the sun shone so fiercely that every morning there was a little less water in the lake and a little more
mud on the bank. The water lilies around the edge began to
droop, and the palms to hang their heads, and the ducks' favorite swimming place, where they could dive the deepest, to
grow shallower and shallower. At length there came a morning when the ducks looked at each other uneasily, and before
nightfall they had whispered that if at the end of two days
rain had not come, they must fly away and seek a new home,
for if they stayed in their old one, which they loved so much,
they would certainly die of thirst.

Earnestly they watched the sky for many hours before they tucked their heads under their wings and fell asleep from sheer weariness, but not the tiniest cloud was to be seen covering the stars that shone so big and brilliant, and hung so low in the heavens they felt they could touch them. So, when the morning broke, they made up their minds they must go and tell the turtle of their plans and bid him farewell.

They found him comfortably curled up on a pile of dead rushes, more than half asleep, for he was old, and could not venture out in the heat as he once did.

'Ah, here you are!' he cried. 'I began to wonder if I was ever going to see you again, for somehow, though the lake has grown smaller, I seem to have grown weaker, and it is lonely spending all day and night by oneself!'

'Oh, my friend,' answered the elder of the two ducks, 'if you have suffered we have suffered also. Besides, I have something to tell you that I fear will cause you greater pain still. If we do not wish to die of thirst, we must leave this place at once and seek another where the sun's rays do not come. My heart bleeds to say this, for there is nothing—nothing else in the world—which would have induced us to separate from you.'

The turtle was so astonished as well as so distressed at the duck's speech that for a moment he could find no words to reply. But when he had forced back his tears, he said in a sad voice:

'How can you think I am able to live without you, when for so long you have been my only friends? If you leave me, death will speedily put an end to my grief.'

'Our sorrow is as great as yours,' answered the other duck, 'but what can we do? And remember that if we are not here to drink the water, there will be the more for you! If it had not been for this terrible misfortune, be sure nothing would have parted us from one we love so dearly.'

'My friends,' replied the turtle, 'water is as necessary to me as to you, and if death stares in your faces, it stares in mine also. But in the name of all the years we have passed together, do not, I beseech you, leave me to perish here alone! Wherever you may go, take me with you!'

There was a pause. The ducks felt wretched at the thought of abandoning their old comrade, yet how could they grant his prayer? It seemed quite impossible, and at length one of them spoke:

'Oh, how can I find words to refuse?' cried he. 'Yet how can we do what you ask? Consider that, like yours, our bodies are heavy and our feet small. Therefore, how could we walk with you over mountains and deserts, till we reached a land where the sun's rays no longer burn? Why, before the day was out we should all three be dead of fatigue and hunger! No, our only hope lies in our wings—and, alas, you cannot fly!'

'No, I cannot fly, of course,' answered the turtle, with a sigh. 'But you are so clever, and have seen so much of the world—surely you can think of some plan?'

Now, the ducks were touched, and making a sign to their friend that they wished to be alone, they swam out into the lake to consult together. Though he could not hear what they said, the turtle could watch, and the half hour their talk lasted felt to him like a hundred years. At length he beheld them returning side by side, and so great was his anxiety to know his fate he almost died from excitement before they reached him.

'We hope we have found a plan that may do for you,' said

the big duck gravely, 'but we must warn you it is not without great danger, especially if you are not careful to follow our directions.'

'How is it possible I should not follow your directions when my life and happiness are at stake?' asked the turtle joyfully. 'Tell me what they are, and I will promise to obey them gratefully.'

'Well, then,' answered the duck, 'while we are carrying you through the air, in the manner we have fixed upon, you must remain as quiet as if you were dead. However high above the earth you may find yourself, you must not feel afraid, nor move your feet, nor open your mouth. No matter what you see or hear, it is absolutely needful for you to be perfectly still, or we cannot answer for the consequences.'

'I will be absolutely obedient,' answered the turtle, 'not only on this occasion but during all my life; and once more I promise faithfully not to move head or foot, to fear nothing, and never to speak a word during the whole journey.'

This being settled, the ducks swam about till they found, floating in the lake, a good stout stick. This they tied to their necks, with some of the tough water-lily roots, and returned as quickly as they could to the turtle.

'Now,' said the elder duck, pushing the stick gently toward his friend, 'take this stick firmly in your mouth, and do not let it go till we have set you down on earth again.'

The turtle did as he was told, and the ducks in their turn seized the stick by the two ends, spread their wings and mounted swiftly into the air, the turtle hanging between them.

For a while all went well. They swept across valleys, over great mountains, above ruined cities, but no lake was to be seen anywhere. Still, the turtle had faith in his friends, and bravely hung on to the stick.

At length they saw in the distance a small village, and very soon they were passing over the roofs of the houses. The people were so astonished at the strange sight, that they all—men, women and children—ran out to see it, and cried to each other:

'Look! Look! Behold a miracle! Two ducks supporting a turtle! Was ever such a thing known before!' Indeed, so great was the surprise that men left their plowing and women their weaving in order to add their voices to their friends'.

The ducks flew steadily on, heeding nothing of the commotion below, but not so the turtle. At first he kept silence as he had been bidden to do, but at length the clamor below proved too much for him, and he began to think everyone was envying him the power of traveling through the air. In an evil moment he forgot the promises he had made so solemnly and opened his mouth to reply. Before he could utter a word, he was rushing so swiftly through the air that he became unconscious, and in this state was dashed to pieces against the side of a house. Then the ducks let the stick fall after him. Sadly they looked at each other and shook their heads.

'We feared it would end so,' said they, 'yet, perhaps, he was right after all. Certainly this death was better than the one that awaited him.'

[From *Les Contes et Fables Indiennes,* par M. Galland, 1724.]

The Snake Prince

ONCE UPON A TIME
there lived by herself, in a city, an old woman who was des-
perately poor. One day she found that she had only a handful
of flour left in the house, and no money to buy more nor hope
of earning it. Carrying her little brass pot, she made her way
down to the river to bathe and to obtain water to make herself
an unleavened cake of what flour she had left. After that she
did not know what was to become of her.

While she was bathing she left her little brass pot on the
river bank covered with a cloth, to keep the inside nice and
clean. But when she took the cloth off the pot she saw inside
it the glittering folds of a deadly snake. Then she said to
herself:

'Ah, kind death! I will take you home to my house, and
there I will shake you out of my pot and you shall bite me and
I will die, and then all my troubles will be ended.'

With these sad thoughts the poor old woman hurried home,
holding her cloth carefully in the mouth of the pot. She shut
all the doors and windows, and took away the cloth and turned
the pot upside down upon her hearthstone. What was her
surprise to find that, instead of the deadly snake which she

expected to see, there fell out with a rattle and a clang a most magnificent necklace of flashing jewels!

For a few minutes she could hardly think or speak, but stood staring. Then with trembling hands she picked the necklace up, and folding it in the corner of her veil, she hurried off to the king's hall of public audience.

'A petition, O King!' she said. 'A petition for your private ear alone!' And when her prayer had been granted, and she found herself alone with the king, she shook out her veil at his feet, and in glittering coils, the splendid necklace fell from it. As soon as the king saw it he was filled with amazement and delight, and the more he looked at it the more he felt he must possess it at once. So he gave the old woman five hundred silver pieces and put the necklace straightway into his pocket. Away she went full of happiness, for the money the king had given her was enough to keep her for the rest of her life.

As soon as he could leave his business the king hurried off and showed his wife his prize, with which she was as pleased as he, if not more so. When they had finished admiring the wonderful necklace, they locked it up in the great chest where the queen's jewelery was kept, the key of which always hung round the king's neck.

A short while afterward, a neighboring king sent a message to say a most lovely girl baby had been born to him. He invited his neighbors to come to a great feast in honor of the occasion. The queen told her husband that of course they must be present at the banquet, and she would wear the new necklace which he had given her.

They had only a short time to prepare for the journey, and at the last moment the king went to the jewel chest but he could see no necklace at all, only in its place, a fat little boy

baby crowing and shouting. The king was so astonished he nearly fell backward, but presently he found his voice. His wife came running, thinking the necklace must at least have been stolen.

'Look here! Look!' cried the king. 'Haven't we always longed for a son? And now Heaven has sent us one!'

'What do you mean?' cried the queen.

The king, danced in excitement round the open chest. 'Come here, and look! Look what we have instead of that necklace!'

Just then the baby let out a great crow of joy, as though he would like to jump up and dance with the king. The queen gave a cry of surprise, and ran to look into the chest.

'Oh!' she gasped, as she looked at the baby. 'What a darling! Where could he have come from?'

'I'm sure I can't say,' said the king. 'All I know is that we locked up a necklace in the chest, and when I unlocked it just now there was no necklace, but a baby, and as fine a baby as ever was seen.'

By this time the queen had the baby in her arms. 'Oh, the

blessed one!' she cried. 'Fairer ornament for the bosom of a
queen than any necklace that ever was wrought. Write,' she
continued, 'write to our neighbor and say that we cannot come
to his feast, for we have a feast of our own and a baby of our
own! Oh, happy day!'

So the visit was given up, and in honor of the new baby,
the bells of the city, its guns and its trumpets, and its people,
small and great, had hardly any rest for a week. There was
such a ringing and banging and blaring, and such fireworks,
feasting and rejoicing, and merrymaking, as had never been
seen before.

A few years went by, and as the king's boy baby and his
neighbor's girl baby grew and throve, the two kings arranged
that as soon as they were old enough they should marry. And
so, with much signing of papers and agreements, and wagging
of wise heads, and stroking of gray beards, the compact was
made, signed and sealed, and lay waiting for its fulfillment.
And this too came to pass, for, as soon as the prince and princess were eighteen years of age, the kings agreed that it was
time for the wedding. The young prince journeyed away to
the neighboring kingdom for his bride, and was there married
to her with great and renewed rejoicings.

Now the old woman who had sold the king the necklace
had been called in by him to be the nurse of the young prince.
Although she loved her charge dearly and was a most faithful
servant, she could not help talking just a little, and so, by-and-
by, it began to be rumored there was some magic about the
young prince's birth. This rumor came in due time to the ears
of the parents of the princess. So now that she was going to be
the wife of the prince, her mother (who was curious, as many
other people are) said to her daughter on the eve of the ceremony:

'Remember, the first thing you must do is to find out what this story is about the prince. You must not speak a word to him, whatever he says, until he asks you why you are silent. Then you must ask him what the truth is about his magic birth, and until he tells you, you must not speak to him again.'

The princess promised she would follow her mother's advice.

Therefore when they were married, and the prince spoke to his bride, she did not answer him. He could not think what was the matter, but even about her old home she would not utter a word. At last he asked why she would not speak; and then she said:

'Tell me the secret of your birth.'

Then the prince was very sad and displeased, and although she pressed him sorely, he would not tell, but always replied, 'If I tell you, you will repent that ever you asked me.'

For several months they lived together, and it was not such a happy time for either as it ought to have been, for the secret was still a secret and lay between them like a cloud between the sun and the earth, making what should be fair, dull and sad.

At length the prince could bear it no longer; so he said to his wife one day, 'At midnight I will tell you my secret if you still wish it; but you will repent it all your life.' However, the princess was overjoyed that she had succeeded and paid no attention to his warnings.

That night the prince ordered horses to be ready for the princess and himself a little before midnight. He placed her on one, mounted the other himself, and they rode together down to the river to the place where the old woman had first found the snake in her brass pot. There the prince drew rein and said sadly:

'Do you still insist that I should tell you my secret?'

And the princess answered, 'Yes.'

'If I do,' answered the prince, 'remember that you will regret it all your life.'

But the princess only replied, 'Tell me!'

'Then,' said the prince, 'know that I am the son of the king of a far country, but by enchantment I was turned into a snake.'

The word 'snake' was hardly out of his lips when he disappeared, and the princess heard a rustle and saw a ripple on the water, and in the faint moonlight she beheld a snake swimming in the river. Soon it disappeared and she was left alone. In vain she waited with beating heart for something to happen, and for the prince to come back to her. Nothing happened and no one came; only the wind mourned through the trees on the river bank, the night birds cried, a jackal howled in the distance, and the river flowed black and silent beneath her.

In the morning they found her, weeping and disheveled, on the river bank, but no word could they learn from her or from anyone of the fate of her husband. At her wish they built a little house of black stone on the river bank, and there she lived in mourning, with a few servants and guards to watch over her.

A long, long time passed by, and still the princess lived in mourning for her prince, saw no one and went nowhere away from her house on the river bank and the garden that surrounded it. One morning, when she woke up, she found a stain of fresh mud upon the carpet.

She sent for the guards, who watched outside the house day and night, and asked them who had entered her room while she was asleep. They declared that no one could have entered, for they kept such careful watch that not even a bird could fly in without their knowledge. But none of them could explain the stain of mud.

At midnight the princess saw a snake wriggling along the floor

The next morning, again the princess found another stain of wet mud, and she questioned everyone most carefully. But none could say how the mud came there. The third night the princess determined to lie awake herself and watch, and for fear she might fall asleep, she cut her finger with a penknife and rubbed salt into the cut that the pain of it might keep her from sleeping.

So she lay awake, and at midnight she saw a snake come wriggling along the floor with some mud from the river in its mouth. When it came near the bed, it reared up and dropped its muddy head on the bedclothes.

She was very frightened, but tried to control her fear, and called out, 'Who are you, and what do you here?'

And the snake answered, 'I am the prince, your husband, and I am come to visit you.'

Then the princess began to weep. The snake continued, 'Alas, did I not say that if I told you my secret you would repent it? And have you not repented?'

'Oh, indeed,' cried the poor princess, 'I have repented it, and shall repent it all my life! Is there nothing I can do?'

And the snake answered, 'Yes, there is one thing, if you dared to do it.'

'Only tell me,' said the princess, 'and I will do anything!'

'Then,' replied the snake, 'on a certain night you must put a large bowl of milk and sugar in each of the four corners of this room. All the snakes in the river will come out to drink the milk, and the one that leads the way will be the queen of the snakes. You must stand in her way at the door, and say, "Oh, Queen of Snakes, Queen of Snakes, give me back my husband!" Perhaps she will do it. But if you are frightened and do not stop her, you will never see me again.' And he glided away.

On the night of which the snake had told her, the princess took four large bowls of milk and sugar and put one in each corner of the room. Then she stood in the doorway waiting. At midnight there was a great hissing and rustling from the direction of the river, and presently the ground appeared to be alive with horrible writhing forms of snakes, whose eyes glittered and forked tongues quivered as they moved on in the direction of the princess' house. Foremost among them was a huge, repulsive scaly creature that led the dreadful procession.

The guards were so terrified they all ran away, but the princess stood in the doorway, as white as death, and with her hands clasped tight together, for fear she should scream or faint and fail to do her part. As they came closer and saw her in the way, all the snakes raised their horrid heads and swayed them to and fro, looking at her with wicked beady eyes, while their breath seemed to poison the very air.

Still the princess stood firm, and when the leading snake was within a few feet of her, she cried, 'Oh, Queen of Snakes, Queen of Snakes, give me back my husband!' Then all the rustling, writhing crowd of snakes seemed to whisper to one another 'Her husband, her husband.' But the queen of snakes moved on until her head was almost in the princess' face, and her little eyes seemed to flash fire. Still the princess stood in the doorway and never moved, but cried again, 'Oh, Queen of Snakes, Queen of Snakes, give me back my husband!'

Then the queen of snakes replied, 'Tomorrow you shall have him—tomorrow!'

When she heard these words and knew that she had conquered, the princess staggered from the door, and sank fainting upon her bed. As in a dream, she saw that her room was full of snakes, all jostling and squabbling over the bowls of milk until it was finished. And then they went away.

In the morning the princess was up early, and took off the mourning dress which she had worn for five whole years and put on gay and beautiful clothes. She swept the house and cleaned it, and adorned it with garlands and nosegays of sweet flowers and ferns, and prepared it as though she were making ready for her wedding. And when night fell she had the woods and gardens lit up with lanterns, and spread a table as for a feast, and in the house a thousand wax candles glowed.

Then the princess waited for her husband, not knowing in what shape he would appear. At midnight the prince came striding from the river laughing, but with tears in his eyes; and she ran to meet him and threw herself into his arms, crying and laughing too.

So the prince came home; and the next day when they two went back to the palace, the old king wept with joy to see them. And the bells, so long silent, were set a-ringing again, the guns firing, the trumpets blaring, and there was fresh feasting and rejoicing.

And the old woman who had been the prince's nurse became nurse to the prince's children—at least she was called so, though she was far too old to do anything for them but love them. Yet she still thought that she was useful and knew that she was happy. And happy, indeed, were the prince and princess, who in due time became king and queen and lived and ruled long and prosperously.

[Major Campbell, Feroshepore.]

The Clever Weaver

ONCE UPON A TIME
the king of a far country was sitting on his throne, listening
to the complaints of his people, and judging between them.
That morning there had been fewer cases than usual to deal
with, and the king was about to rise and go into his gardens,
when a sudden stir was heard outside. The lord high chamberlain entered and inquired if his majesty would be graciously
pleased to receive the ambassador of a powerful emperor who
lived in the east and was greatly feared by the neighboring
sovereigns. The king, who stood as much in dread of him as
the rest, gave orders that the envoy should be admitted at once,
and that a banquet should be prepared in his honor. Then he
seated himself again on his throne, wondering what the envoy
had to say.

The envoy said nothing. He advanced to the throne where
the king was awaiting him, and stooping down, traced a black
circle all round it on the floor. Then he sat down and took no
further notice of anyone.

The king and his courtiers were equally mystified and en-
raged at this strange behavior. But the envoy sat as calm and
still as an image, and it soon became plain that they would

get no explanation from him. The ministers were hastily summoned to a council, but not one of them could throw any light upon the subject. This made the king more angry than ever, and he told them that unless they could find someone capable of solving the mystery before sunset he would hang them all.

The king was, as the ministers knew, a man of his word. They quickly mapped out the city into districts, so they might visit house by house, and question the occupants as to the action of the ambassador. Most of them received no reply to their questions except a puzzled stare. But, luckily, one more observant than the rest, on entering an empty cottage found a swing swinging of itself. He began to think it might be worth while for him to see the owner.

Opening a door, he found a second swing, swinging gently like the first, and from the window he beheld a patch of corn, and a willow which switched perpetually to frighten away the sparrows though there was no wind. Feeling more and more curious, he descended the stairs and found himself in a large light workshop where a weaver sat at his loom. But all the weaver did was to guide his threads, for the machine he had invented to set in motion the swings and the willow pole made the loom work.

When he saw the great wheel standing in the corner, and had guessed the use of it, the minister heaved a sigh of relief. If the weaver could not guess the riddle, he at least might put the minister on the right track. So without more ado he told the story of the circle, and ended by declaring that the person who could explain its meaning should be handsomely rewarded.

'Come with me at once,' he said. 'The sun is low in the heavens and there is no time to lose.'

The weaver stood thinking for a moment and then walked across to a window, outside of which was a hencoop with two knucklebones lying beside it. These he picked up, and taking the hen from the coop, he tucked it under his arm.

'I am ready,' he answered, turning to the minister.

In the hall the king still sat on his throne, and the envoy on his chair. Signing to the minister to remain where he was, the weaver advanced to the envoy and placed the knucklebones on the floor beside him. For answer, the envoy took a handful of millet seed out of his pocket and scattered it round; upon which the weaver set down the hen, who ate it up in a moment. At that the envoy rose without a word and took his departure.

As soon as he had left the hall, the king beckoned to the weaver.

'You alone seem to have guessed the riddle,' said he, 'and great shall be your reward. But tell me, I pray you, what it all means?'

'The meaning, O King,' replied the weaver, 'is this: The circle drawn by the envoy round your throne is the message of the emperor, and signifies, "If I send an army and surround your capital, will you lay down your arms?" The knucklebones which I placed before him told him, "You are but children in comparison with us. Toys like these are the only playthings you are fit for." The millet that he scattered was an emblem of the number of soldiers that his master can bring into the field; but by the hen which ate up the seed he understood that one of our men could destroy a host of theirs. I do not think,' he added, 'that the emperor will declare war.'

'You have saved me and my honor,' cried the king, 'and wealth and glory shall be heaped upon you. Name your reward, and you shall have it even to the half of my kingdom.'

'The small farm outside the city gates, as a marriage portion for my daughter, is all I ask,' answered the weaver, and it was all he would accept. 'Only, O King,' were his parting words, 'I would beg of you to remember that weavers also are of value to a state, and that they are sometimes cleverer even than ministers!'

[From *Contes Arméniens,* par Frédéric Macler.]

He Wins Who Waits

ONCE UPON A TIME
there reigned a king who had an only daughter. The girl had
been spoiled by everybody from her birth. Besides being beautiful she was clever and willful. When she grew old enough
to be married she refused to have anything to say to the prince
her father favored, but declared she would choose a husband
for herself. By long experience the king knew when once she
had made up her mind, there was no use expecting her to
change it, so he inquired meekly what she wished him to do.

'Summon all the young men in the kingdom to appear before
me a month from today,' answered the princess. The one to
whom I give this golden apple shall be my husband.'

'But, my dear—' began the king, in tones of dismay.

'The one to whom I give this golden apple shall be my husband,' repeated the princess, in a louder voice than before.
And the king understood the warning, and with a sigh proceeded to do her bidding.

The young men arrived—tall and short, dark and fair, rich
and poor. They stood in rows in the great courtyard in front
of the palace, and the princess, clad in robes of green, with a
golden veil flowing behind her, passed before them all, holding

the apple. Once or twice she stopped and hesitated, but in the end she always passed on, till she came to a youth near the end of the last row. There was nothing specially remarkable about him, the bystanders thought; nothing that was likely to take a girl's fancy. A hundred others were handsomer, and all wore finer clothes; but he met the princess' eyes frankly and with a smile, and she smiled, too, and held out the apple.

'There is some mistake,' cried the king, who had anxiously watched her progress and hoped that none of the candidates would please her. 'It is impossible that she can wish to marry the son of a poor widow, who has not a farthing in the world! Tell her I will not hear of it and she must go through the rows again and fix upon someone else.'

The princess went through the rows a second and a third time, and on each occasion she gave the apple to the widow's son.

'Well, marry him if you will,' exclaimed the angry king; 'but at least you shall not stay here.' The princess answered nothing, but threw up her head, and taking the widow's son by the hand, she left the castle with him.

That evening they were married and, after the ceremony, went back to the house of the bridegroom's mother which, in the eyes of the princess, did not look much bigger than a hen coop.

The old woman was not at all pleased when her son entered, bringing his bride with him.

'As if we were not poor enough before,' grumbled she. 'I dare say this is some fine lady who can do nothing to earn her living.' But the princess stroked her arm, and said softly:

'Do not be vexed, dear Mother. I am a famous spinner and can sit at my wheel all day without breaking a thread.'

She kept her word. But in spite of the efforts of all three, they became poorer and poorer, and at the end of six months it was agreed that the husband should go to the neighboring town to seek work. A merchant he met was about to start on a long journey, with a train of camels laden with goods of all sorts, and needed a man to help him.

The widow's son begged he would take him as a servant, and to this the merchant assented, giving him his whole year's salary beforehand. The young man returned home with the news, and next day bade farewell to his mother and his wife, who were very sad at parting from him.

'Do not forget me while you are absent,' whispered the princess as she flung her arms round his neck. 'And as you pass by the well, which lies near the city gate, stop and greet the old man you will find sitting there. Kiss his hand, and ask him what counsel he can give you for your journey.'

Then the youth set out, and when he reached the well where the old man was sitting, he asked the question as his wife had bidden him.

'My son,' replied the old man, 'you have done well to come to me, and in return remember three things: "The one whom the heart loves is ever the most beautiful," "Patience is the first step on the road to happiness," "He wins who waits." '

The young man thanked him and went on his way. Next morning early the caravan set out, and before sunset it had arrived at the first halting place, near some wells, where another company of merchants had already encamped. But no rain had fallen for a long while in that rocky country, and both men and beasts were parched with thirst. To be sure, there was another well about half a mile away, where there was always water. But to get it one had to be lowered deep down, and no one who had ever descended that well had been known to come back.

However, till they could store some water in their bags of goatskin, the caravans dared go no farther. The merchants were offering a large reward to anyone brave enough to go down into the enchanted well. At sunrise the young man was aroused from his sleep by a herald, making his round of the camp, proclaiming that every merchant present would give a thousand piastres to the man who would risk his life to bring water.

The youth hesitated for a while when he heard the proclamation. The story of the well had spread far and wide and, long ago, had reached his ears. The danger was great, he knew, but if he came back alive, he would be the possessor of eighty thousand piastres. He turned to the herald who was passing the tent:

'I will go,' said he.

'What madness!' cried his master, who happened to be standing near. 'You are too young to throw away your life like that. Run after the herald and tell him you take back your offer.' But the young man shook his head, and the merchant saw it was useless to try and persuade him.

'Well, it is your own affair,' he observed at last. 'If you must go, you must. Only, if you ever return, I will give you a camel's load of goods and my best mule besides.' And touching his turban in token of farewell, he entered the tent.

Hardly had he done so than a crowd of men were seen pouring out of the camp.

'How can we thank you!' they exclaimed, pressing round the youth. 'Our camels as well as ourselves are almost dead of thirst. See! Here is the rope we have brought to let you down.'

'Come, then,' answered the youth. And they all set out.

On reaching the well, the rope was knotted securely under

his arms, a big goatskin bottle was given him, and he was gently lowered to the bottom of the pit. Here a clear stream was bubbling over the rocks. Stooping down, he was about to drink when a huge Arab appeared before him, saying in a loud voice, 'Come with me!'

The young man rose, never doubting that his last hour had come; but as he could do nothing, he followed the Arab into a brilliantly lighted hall, on the further side of the little river. There his guide sat down, and drawing toward him two boys, he said to the stranger:

'I have a question to ask you. If you answer it right, your life shall be spared. If not, your head will be forfeit, as the head of many another has been before you. Tell me: which of my two children do I think the handsomer.'

The question did not seem a hard one, for while one boy was as beautiful a child as ever was seen, his brother was very ugly. But, just as the youth was going to speak, the old man's counsel flashed into the youth's mind, and he replied hastily, 'The one whom the heart loves is ever the most beautiful.'

'You have saved me!' cried the Arab, rising quickly from his seat, and pressing the young man in his arms. 'Ah, if you could only guess what I have suffered from the stupidity of all the people to whom I have put that question. I was condemned by a wicked genius to remain here until it was answered! But what brought you to this place, and how can I reward you for what you have done for me?'

'By helping me draw enough water for my caravan of eighty merchants and their camels, who are dying for want of it,' replied the youth.

'That is easily done,' said the Arab. 'Take these three apples, and when you have filled your goatskin and are ready to be drawn up, lay one of them on the ground. Halfway to the earth, let fall another, and at the top, drop the third. If you follow my directions no harm will happen to you. And take, besides, these three pomegranates, green, red and white. One day you will find a use for them!'

The young man did as he was told and stepped out on the rocky waste, where the merchants were anxiously awaiting him. Oh, how thirsty they all were! But even after the camels had drunk, the skin seemed as full as ever.

Full of gratitude for their deliverance, the merchants pressed the money into his hands, while his own master bade him choose what goods he liked and a mule to carry them.

So the widow's son was rich at last, and when the merchant had sold his merchandise and returned home to his native city, his servant hired a man by whom he sent the money and the mule back to his wife.

I will send the pomegranates also, thought he, for if I leave them in my turban they may some day fall out, and he drew them forth.

For a long time he remained with the merchant, who gradually trusted him with all his business and gave him a large share of the money he made. When his master died, the young man wished to return home, but the widow begged him to stay and help her; and one day he awoke with a start, to remember that twenty years had passed since he had gone away.

'I want to see my wife,' he said next morning to his mistress. 'If at any time I can be of use to you, send a messenger to me. Meanwhile, I have told Hassan what to do.' And mounting a camel he set out.

Now, soon after he had taken service with the merchant a little boy had been born to him, and both the princess and the old woman toiled hard all day to buy food and clothing for the baby. When the money and the pomegranates arrived there was no need for them to work any more, and the princess saw at once that they were not fruit at all but precious stones of great value. The old woman, however, not being accustomed to the sight of jewels, took them for common fruit and wished to give them to the child to eat. She was very angry when the princess hastily took them from her. The wise young woman hid them in her dress, while she went to the market and bought the three finest pomegranates she could find for the little boy.

Then she bought beautiful new clothes for all of them, and when they were dressed they looked as fine as could be. Next, she took out one of the precious stones and placed it in a small silver box. This she wrapped in a handkerchief embroidered in gold and filled the old woman's pockets with gold and silver pieces.

'Go, dear Mother,' she said, 'to the palace, and present the jewel to the king. If he asks you what he can give you in return, tell him that you want a paper, with his seal attached, proclaiming that no one is to meddle with anything you may choose to do. Before you leave the palace distribute the money amongst the servants.'

The old woman took the box and started for the palace. No one there had ever seen a ruby of such beauty, and the most famous jeweler in the town was summoned to declare its value. But all he could say was:

'If a boy threw a stone into the air with all his might, and you could pile up gold as high as the flight of the stone, it would not be sufficient to pay for this ruby.'

At these words the king's face fell. Having once seen the ruby he could not bear to part with it, yet all the money in his treasury would not be enough to buy it. At last he said:

'If I cannot give you its worth in money, is there anything you will take in exchange?'

'A paper signed by your hand and sealed with your seal, proclaiming that I may do what I will, without let or hindrance,' answered she promptly. And the king, delighted to have obtained what he coveted at so small a cost, gave her the paper without delay. Then the old woman took her leave and returned home.

The fame of this wonderful ruby soon spread far and wide, and envoys arrived at the little house to know if there were more stones to sell. Each king was so anxious to gain possession of the treasure that he bade his messenger outbid all the rest, and so the princess sold the two remaining stones for a sum of money so large that if the gold pieces had been spread out they would have reached from there to the moon.

The first thing she did was to build a palace by the side of the cottage; it was raised on pillars of gold, set with great dia-

The lady was joined by a young man

monds which blazed night and day. Of course the news of this palace was the first thing that reached the king her father, on his return from the wars, and he hurried to see it. In the doorway stood a young man of twenty. The king was so pleased with the appearance of the youth that he carried him back to his own palace and made him commander of the whole army.

Not long after this, the widow's son returned to his native land. There, sure enough, was the tiny cottage where he had lived with his mother, but the gorgeous building beside it was quite new to him. What had become of his wife and his mother, and who could be living in that other wonderful place? Not wishing to betray himself by asking questions of passing strangers, he climbed up into a tree that stood opposite the palace and watched.

By-and-by a lady came out and began to gather some of the roses and jessamine that hung about the porch. The twenty years that had passed since he had last beheld her vanished in an instant, and he knew her to be his own wife, looking almost as young and beautiful as on the day of their parting.

He was about to jump down from the tree and hasten to her side, when she was joined by a young man who placed his arm affectionately round her neck. At this sight the angry husband drew his bow, but before he could let fly the arrow, the counsel of the wise man came back to him: 'Patience is the first step on the road to happiness.' And he laid it down again.

At this moment the princess turned and, drawing her companion's head down to hers, kissed him on each cheek. A second time blind rage filled the heart of the watcher and he snatched up his bow from the branch where it hung, when words, heard long since, seemed to sound in his ears, 'He wins who waits.' And the bow dropped to his side.

Then, through the silent air came the sound of the youth's voice, 'Mother, can you tell me nothing about my father? Does he still live and will he ever return to us?'

'Alas, my son, how can I answer you?' replied the lady. 'Twenty years have passed since he left us to make his fortune, and in that time, only once have I heard aught of him. But what has brought him to your mind just now?'

'Because last night I dreamed he was here,' said the youth, 'and then I remembered what I have so long forgotten, that I had a father, though even his very history was strange to me. And now, tell me, I pray you, all you can concerning him.'

And standing under the jessamine, the son learned his father's history, and the man in the tree listened also.

'Oh,' exclaimed the youth, when the tale was ended, while he twisted his hands in pain, 'I am general-in-chief, you are the king's daughter, and we have the most splendid palace in the whole world, yet my father lives we know not where and, for all we can guess, may be poor and miserable. Tomorrow I will ask the king to give me soldiers, and I will seek him over the whole earth till I find him.'

Then the man came down from the tree and clasped his wife and son in his arms. All that night they talked, and when the sun rose it found them still talking. As soon as it was proper, he went up to the palace to pay his homage to the king and to inform him of all that had happened and who they all really were. The king was overjoyed to think that his daughter, whom he had long since forgiven and sorely missed, was living at his gates, and was, besides, the mother of the youth who was so dear to him.

'It was written beforehand!' cried the monarch. 'You are my son-in-law before the world, and shall be king after me.'

And the man bowed his head.

He had waited, and he had won.

[From *Contes Arméniens,* par Frédéric Macler.]

The Silent Princess

ONCE UPON A TIME there lived in Turkey a pasha who had only one son, and so dearly did he love this boy that he let him spend the whole day amusing himself, instead of learning how to be useful.

Now the boy's favorite toy was a golden ball, and with this he would play from morning till night, without troubling anybody. One day, as he was sitting in the summerhouse, making his ball run all along the walls and catching it again, he noticed an old woman with an earthen pitcher coming to draw water from a well in a corner of the garden. In a moment he had caught his ball and flung it straight at the pitcher, which fell to the ground in a thousand pieces. The old woman started with surprise, but said nothing; only turned round to fetch another pitcher, and as soon as she had disappeared, the boy hurried out to pick up his ball.

Scarcely was he back in the summerhouse when he beheld the old woman a second time, approaching the well with the pitcher on her shoulder. She had just taken hold of the handle to lower it into the water, when—crash—the pitcher lay in fragments at her feet! Of course she felt very angry, but for fear of the pasha she still held her peace and spent her last pence in buying a fresh pitcher. But when this, too, was broken by a blow from the ball, her wrath burst forth, and shaking her fist toward the summerhouse where the boy was hiding, she cried:

'I wish you may be punished by falling in love with the silent princess.' And having said this she vanished.

For some time the boy paid no heed to her words—indeed he forgot them altogether. But as years went by, and he began to think more about things, the remembrance of the old woman's wish came back to his mind.

'Who is the silent princess? And why should it be a punishment to fall in love with her?' he asked himself and received no answer. However, that did not prevent him from putting the question again and again, till at length he grew so weak and ill he could eat nothing, and in the end was forced to lie in bed altogether. His father became so frightened by this strange disease, that he sent for every physician in the kingdom to cure him, but no one was able to find a remedy.

'How did your illness first begin, my son?' asked the pasha one day. 'Perhaps, if we knew that, we should also know better what to do for you.'

Then the youth told him what had happened all those years before, when he was a little boy, and what the old woman had said to him.

'Give me, I pray you,' he cried, when his tale was finished, 'leave to go through the world in search of the princess and perhaps this evil state may cease.'

Sore though his heart was to part from his only son, the pasha felt sure the young man would certainly die if he remained at home any longer.

'Go, and peace be with you,' he answered. And he called his

trusted steward, whom he ordered to accompany his young master.

Their preparations were soon made, and early one morning the two set out. First they lost their way in a dense forest, and from that they at length emerged into a wilderness where they wandered for six months, not seeing a living creature and finding scarcely anything to eat or drink. They became nothing but skin and bone, while their garments hung in tatters about them.

They had forgotten all about the princess, and their only wish was to find themselves back in the palace again when, one day, they found they were on the shoulder of a mountain. The stones beneath them shone as brightly as diamonds, and their hearts beat with joy at beholding a tiny old man approaching them. The sight awoke all manner of recollections; the numb feeling that had taken possession of them fell away as if by magic, and it was with glad voices they greeted the new-comer.

'Where are we, my friend?' asked they. The old man told them the mountain was near where the sultan's daughter sat, covered by seven veils, and the shining of the stones was only the reflection of her own brilliance.

On hearing this news all the dangers and difficulties of their past wandering vanished from their minds.

'How can I reach her?' asked the youth eagerly.

But the old man only answered, 'Have patience, my son, yet awhile. Another six months must go by before you arrive at the palace where she dwells with the rest of the women. And, even so, think well while you can, for should you fail to make her speak, you will have to pay forfeit with your life, as others have done. So beware!'

But the prince only laughed at this counsel—as others had also done.

AFTER three months they found themselves on the top of another mountain, and the prince saw with surprise that its sides were colored a beautiful red. Perched on some cliffs, not far off, was a small village, and the prince proposed to his friend that they should go and rest there. The villagers, on their part, welcomed them gladly and gave them food to eat and beds to sleep on, and thankful indeed were the two travelers to repose their weary limbs.

The next morning they asked their host if he could tell them whether they were still many days' journey from the princess, and whether he knew why the mountain was so much redder than other mountains.

'For three and a half more months you must still pursue your way,' answered he, 'and by that time you will find yourselves at the gate of the princess' palace. As for the color of the mountain, that comes from the soft hue of her cheeks and mouth, which shines through the seven veils which cover her. But none have ever beheld her face, for she sits there, uttering no word, though one hears whispers of many having lost their lives for her sake.'

The prince, however, would listen no further. Thanking the man for his kindness, he jumped up and, with the steward, set out to climb the mountain.

On and on and on they went, sleeping under the trees or in caves, and living upon berries and any fish they could catch in the rivers. But at length, when their clothes were nearly in rags and their legs so tired they could hardly walk any farther, they saw on the top of the next mountain a palace of yellow marble.

'There it is, at last!' cried the prince. And fresh blood seemed to spring in his veins. But as he and his companion began to climb toward the top they paused in horror, for the ground was white with skulls. The prince recovered his voice first, and he said to his friend, as carelessly as he could:

'These must be the skulls of the men who tried to make the princess speak and failed. Well, if we fail too, our bones will strew the ground likewise.'

'Oh, turn back now, my Prince, while there is yet time,' entreated his companion. 'Your father gave you into my charge, but when we set out I did not know that certain death lay before us.'

'Take heart, O Lala, take heart!' answered the prince. 'A man can but die once. And, besides, the princess will have to speak some day, you know.'

So they went on again, and by-and-by they reached another village where they determined to rest for a little while so their wits might be fresh and bright for the task before them. But this time, though the people were kind and friendly, their faces were gloomy, and every now and then woeful cries would rend the air.

'Oh, my brother, have I lost you?' 'Oh, my son, shall I see you no more?'

The young man stood thoughtful for a short time. Then, turning to the lala, he said:

'Well, our destiny will soon be decided! Meanwhile we will find out all we can, and do nothing rashly.'

For two or three days they wandered about the bazaars, keeping their eyes and ears open, when one morning, they met a man carrying a nightingale in a cage. The bird was singing so joyously that the prince stopped to listen and at once offered to buy her.

'Oh, why cumber yourself with such a useless thing?' cried the lala in disgust. 'Have you not enough to occupy your hands and mind, without taking an extra burden?'

But the prince, who liked having his own way, paid no heed to him. Paying the high price asked by the man, he carried the bird back to the inn and hung her up in his chamber. That evening, as he was sitting alone, trying to think of something that would make the princess talk, and failing altogether, the nightingale pecked open her cage door, which was lightly fastened by a stick. Perching on his shoulder, she murmured softly in his ear:

'What makes you so sad, my Prince?'

The young man started. In his native country birds did not talk, and like many people, he was always rather afraid of what he did not understand. But in a moment he felt ashamed of his folly, and explained that he had traveled for more than a year, over thousands of miles, to win the hand of the sultan's daughter. And now that he had reached his goal he could think of no plan to force her to speak.

'Oh, do not trouble your head about that,' replied the bird, 'it is quite easy! Go this evening to the women's apartments, and take me with you, and when you enter the princess' private chamber hide me under the pedestal which supports the great golden candlestick. The princess herself will be wrapped so thickly in her seven veils that she can see nothing, neither can her face be seen by anyone. Then inquire after her health, but she will remain silent. Next say that you are sorry to have disturbed her and that you will have a little talk with the pedestal of the candlestick. When you speak I will answer.'

The prince threw his mantle over the bird and started for the palace, where he begged an audience of the sultan. This was soon granted him, and leaving the nightingale, hidden by the mantle, in a dark corner outside the door, he walked up to the throne on which his highness was sitting, and bowed low before him.

'What is your request?' asked the sultan, looking closely at the young man, who was tall and handsome. But when he heard the tale he shook his head pityingly.

'If you can make her speak she shall be your wife,' answered he. 'But if not—did you mark the skulls that strewed the mountainside?'

'Some day a man is bound to break the spell, O Sultan,' replied the youth boldly, 'and why should it not be I as well as another? At any rate, my word is pledged; I cannot draw back now.'

'Well, go if you must,' said the sultan. And he bade his attendants lead the way to the chamber of the princess, but to allow the young man to enter alone.

Catching up, unseen, his mantle and the cage as they passed into the dark corridor—for by this time night was coming on—the youth found himself standing in a room bare except

for a pile of silken cushions, and one tall golden candlestick.
His heart beat high as he looked at the cushions, and knew
that, shrouded within the shining veils that covered them, lay
the much longed-for princess.

Then, fearful that other eyes might be watching him, he
hastily placed the nightingale under the open pedestal on which
the candlestick was resting, and turning again, he steadied his
voice and besought the princess to tell him of her well-being.

Not by even a movement of her hand did the princess show
she had heard, and the young man, who of course expected
this, went on to speak of his travels and of the strange
countries he had passed through. But not a sound broke her
silence.

'I see clearly that you are interested in none of these things,'
said he at last, 'and as I have been forced to hold my peace
for so many months, I feel that now I really must talk to somebody, so I shall go and address my conversation to the candlestick.' And with that he crossed the room behind the princess,
and cried, 'O fairest of candlesticks, how are you?'

'Very well indeed, my lord,' answered the nightingale; 'but
I wonder how many years have gone by since any one has
spoken with me. Now that you have come, rest awhile, I pray
you, and listen to my story.'

'Willingly,' replied the youth, curling himself up on the
floor, for there was no cushion for him to sit on.

'Once upon a time,' began the nightingale, 'there lived a
pasha whose daughter was the most beautiful maiden in the
whole kingdom. Suitors she had in plenty, but she was not easy
to please, and at length there were only three she felt she could
even think of marrying. Not knowing which of the three she
liked best, she took counsel with her father, who summoned
the young men into his presence and told them that each must

'O fairest of candlesticks, how are you?'

learn some trade, and whichever of them proved the cleverest at the end of six months should become the husband of the princess.

'Though the three suitors may have been secretly disappointed, they could not help feeling that this test was quite fair, and left the palace together, talking as they went of what handicrafts they might set themselves to follow. The day was hot, and when they reached a spring that gushed out of the side of the mountain, they stopped to drink and rest, and then one of them said:

' "It will be best that we should each seek our fortunes alone; so let us put our rings under this stone and go our separate ways. The first one who returns hither will take his ring, and the others will take theirs. Thus we shall know whether we have all fulfilled the commands of the pasha, or if some accident has befallen any of us."

' "Good," replied the other two. And the three rings were placed in a little hole, carefully covered again by the stone.

'Then they parted, and for six months they knew naught of each other till, on the day appointed, they met at the spring. Right glad they all were, and eagerly they talked of what they had done and how the time had been spent.

' "I think I shall win the princess," said the eldest, with a laugh, "for it is not everybody who is able to accomplish a whole year's journey in an hour!"

' "That is very clever, certainly," answered his friend. "But if you are to govern a kingdom it may be still more useful to have the power of seeing what is happening at a distance; and that is what I have learned," replied the second.

' "No, no, my dear comrades," cried the third, "your trades are all very well; but when the pasha hears that I can bring back the dead to life he will know which of us is to be his son-in-law. But come, there only remain a few hours of the six months he granted us. It is time that we hastened back to the palace."

' "Stop a moment," said the second, "it would be well to know what is going on in the palace." And plucking some small leaves from a tree near by, he muttered some words and made some signs, and laid them on his eyes. In an instant he turned pale and uttered a cry.

' "What is it? What is it?" exclaimed the others; and, with a shaking voice, he gasped:

' "The princess is lying on her bed, and has barely a few minutes to live. Oh! Can no one save her?"

' "I can," answered the third, taking a small box from his turban; "this ointment will cure any illness. But how to reach her in time?"

' "Give it to me," said the first. And he wished himself by the bedside of the princess, which was surrounded by the sultan and his weeping courtiers. Clearly there was not a second to lose, for the princess was unconscious and her face cold. Plunging his finger into the ointment he touched her eyes, mouth and ears with the paste, and with beating heart awaited the result.

'It was swifter than he supposed. As he looked the color came back into her cheeks, and she smiled up at her father. The sultan, almost speechless with joy at this sudden change, embraced his daughter tenderly, and then turned to the young man to whom he owed her life:

' "Are you not one of the three I sent forth to learn a trade six months ago?" asked he. And the young man answered yes, and that the other two were even now on their way to the palace so the sultan might judge between them.'

At this point in her story the nightingale stopped, and asked the prince which of the three he thought had the best right to the princess.

'The one who had learned how to prepare the ointment,' replied he.

'But if it had not been for the man who could see what was happening at a distance they would never have known the princess was ill,' said the nightingale. 'I would give it to him.' And the argument between them waxed hot till, suddenly, the listening princess started up from her cushions and cried:

'Oh, you fools! Cannot you understand that if it had not been for him who had power to reach the palace in time the ointment itself would have been useless, for death would have claimed her? It is he and no other who ought to have the princess!'

At the first sound of the princess' voice a slave, who was standing at the door, ran at full speed to tell the sultan of the miracle, and the delighted father hastened to the spot. But by this time the princess perceived she had fallen into a trap, cunningly laid for her, and would not utter another word. She made signs to her father that the man who wished to be her husband must induce her to speak three times. And she smiled to herself beneath her seven veils as she thought of the impossibility of that.

When the sultan told the prince that, though he had succeeded once, he would have twice to pass through the same test, the young man's face clouded over. It did not seem to him fair play, but he dared not object. He only bowed low and contrived to step back close to the spot where the nightingale was hidden. Unseen he tucked the little cage under his cloak and left the palace.

'Why are you so gloomy?' asked the nightingale, as soon as they were safely outside. 'Everything has gone exactly right!

Of course the princess was very angry with herself for having spoken. And did you see that, at her first words, the veils covering her began to rend? Take me back tomorrow evening and place me on the pillar by the lattice. Fear nothing, you have only to trust to me!'

The next evening, toward sunset, the prince left the cage behind him, and with the bird in the folds of his garment slipped into the palace and made his way straight to the princess' apartments. He was at once admitted by the slaves who guarded the door and took care to pass near the window so the nightingale could hop unseen to the top of a pillar. Then he turned and bowed low to the princess. He asked her several questions, but as before, she answered nothing, and indeed, gave no sign that she heard. After a few minutes the young man bowed again, and crossing over to the window, he said:

'Oh, pillar! It is no use speaking to the princess, she will not utter one word, and as I must talk to somebody, I have come to you. Tell me how you have been all this long while?'

'I thank you,' replied a voice from the pillar, 'I am feeling very well. And it is lucky for me that the princess is silent, else you would not have wanted to speak to me. To reward you, I will relate to you an interesting tale I lately overheard and about which I should like to have your opinion.'

'That will be charming,' answered the prince, 'so pray begin at once.'

'Once upon a time,' said the nightingale, 'there lived a woman who was so beautiful that every man who saw her fell in love with her. But she was very hard to please and refused to wed any of them, though she managed to keep friends with all. Years passed away, almost without her noticing. One by one the young men grew tired of waiting and sought wives who may have been less handsome, but were also less proud.

At length, only three of her former wooers remained—Baldschi, Jagdschi and Firedschi. Still she held herself apart, thought herself better and lovelier than other women, when, on a certain evening, her eyes were opened at last to the truth. She was sitting before her mirror, combing her curls, when amongst her raven locks she found a long white hair!

'At this dreadful sight her heart gave a jump and then stood still.

' "I am growing old," she said to herself, "and if I do not choose a husband soon, I shall never have one! I know that one of those three men would gladly marry me tomorrow, but I cannot decide between them. I must invent some way to find out which of them is the best, and lose no time about it."

'So instead of going to sleep, she thought all night long of different plans, and in the morning she rose and dressed herself.

' "That will have to do," she muttered as she pulled out the white hair which had cost her so much trouble. "It is not very good, but I can think of nothing better; and—well, they are none of them clever, and I dare say they will easily fall into the trap." Then she called her slave and bade her let Jagdschi know that she would be ready to receive him in an hour's time. After that she went into the garden and dug a grave under a tree, by which she laid a white shroud.

'Jagdschi was delighted with the gracious message, and putting on his newest garments, he hastened to the lady's house, but great was his dismay at finding her stretched on her cushions, weeping bitterly.

' "What is the matter, O Fair One?" he asked, bowing low before her.

' "A terrible thing has happened," said she, her voice choked with sobs. "My father died two nights ago and I buried him in my garden. But now I find that he was a wizard and was not dead at all, for his grave is empty, and he is wandering about somewhere in the world."

' "That is evil news indeed," answered Jagdschi; "but can I do nothing to comfort you?"

' "There is one thing you can do," replied she, "wrap yourself in the shroud and lay yourself in the grave. If he should not return till after three hours have elapsed he will have lost his power over me and be forced to go and wander elsewhere."

'Now Jagdschi was proud of the trust reposed in him, and wrapping himself in the shroud, he stretched himself at full length in the grave. After some time Baldschi arrived in his turn, and found the lady groaning and lamenting. She told him that her father had been a wizard, and that in case, as was very likely, he should wish to leave his grave and come to work her evil, Baldschi was to take a stone and be ready to crush in his head.

'Baldschi, enchanted at being able to do his lady a service, picked up a stone, and seated himself by the side of the grave wherein lay Jagdschi.

Meanwhile the hour arrived in which Firedschi was accustomed to pay his respects, and as in the case of the other two he discovered the lady overcome with grief. To him she said that a wizard who was an enemy of her father's had thrown the dead man out of his grave and had taken his place.

"But," she added, "if you can bring the wizard into my presence, all his power will go from him; if not, then I am lost."

' "Ah, lady, what is there I would not do for you!" cried Firedschi, and running down to the grave, he seized the astonished Jagdschi by the waist. Flinging the body over his shoulder, he hastened with him into the house. At the first moment Baldschi was so surprised at this turn of affairs, for which the lady had not prepared him, that he sat still and did nothing. But by-and-by he sprang up and hurled the stone after the two flying figures, hoping it might kill them both. Fortunately it touched neither, and soon all three were in the presence of the lady. Then Jagdschi, thinking he had delivered her from the power of the wizard, slid off the back of Firedschi, and threw the shroud from him.'

'Tell me, my Prince,' said the nightingale, when she had finished her story, 'which of the three men deserved to win the lady? I myself should choose Firedschi.'

'No, no,' answered the prince, who understood the wink the bird had given him; 'it was Baldschi who took the most trouble, and it was certainly he who deserved the lady.'

But the nightingale would not agree; and they began to quarrel, till a third voice broke in:

'How can you talk such nonsense?' cried the princess—and as she spoke a sound of tearing was heard. 'Why, you have never even thought of Jagdschi, who lay for three hours in the grave, with a stone held over his head! Of course the lady chose him for her husband!'

It was not many minutes before the news reached the sultan; but even now he would not consent to the marriage till his daughter had spoken a third time. On hearing this, the young man took counsel with the nightingale. The bird told him that as the princess, in her fury at having fallen into the snare laid for her, had ordered the pillar broken in pieces, she must be hidden in the folds of a curtain that hung by the door.

The following evening the prince entered the palace, and walked boldly up to the princess' apartments. As he entered, the nightingale flew from under his arm and perched herself on top of the door, where she was entirely concealed by the folds of the dark curtain. The young man talked as usual to the princess without obtaining a single word in reply, and at length he left her lying under the heap of shining veils—now rent in many places—and crossed the room toward the door, from which a voice gladly answered him.

For a while the two talked together: then the nightingale asked if the prince was fond of stories, as she had lately heard one which interested and perplexed her greatly. In reply, the prince begged that he might hear it at once, and without further delay the nightingale began:

'Once upon a time, a carpenter, a tailor and a student set out together to see the world. After wandering about for some months they grew tired of traveling, and resolved to stay and rest in a small town that took their fancy. So they hired a little house and looked about for work to do, returning at sunset to smoke their pipes and talk over the events of the day.

'One night in the middle of summer it was hotter than usual, and the carpenter found himself unable to sleep. Instead of tossing about on his cushions, making himself more uncomfortable than he was already, the man wisely got up, drank some coffee and lit his long pipe. Suddenly his eye fell on some pieces of wood in a corner, and being very clever with his fingers, he had soon set up a perfect statue of a girl about fourteen years old. This so pleased and quieted him that he grew quite drowsy, and going back to bed fell fast asleep.

'But the carpenter was not the only person who lay awake that night. Thunder was in the air, and the tailor became so restless that he thought he would go downstairs and cool his feet in the little fountain outside the garden door. To reach the door he had to pass through the room where the carpenter had sat and smoked, and against the wall he beheld a beautiful girl. He stood speechless for an instant before he ventured to touch her hand, when to his amazement, he found she was fashioned out of wood.

' "Ah! I can make you more beautiful still," said he. And fetching from a shelf a roll of yellow silk which he had bought that day from a merchant, he cut and draped and stitched, till at length a lovely robe clothed the slender figure. When this was finished, the restlessness had departed from him and he went back to bed.

'As dawn approached the student arose and prepared to go to the mosque with the first ray of sunlight. But when he saw the maiden standing there, he fell on his knees and lifted his hands in ecstasy.

' "Oh, you are fairer than the evening air, clad in the beauty of ten thousand stars," he murmured to himself. "Surely a form so rare was never meant to live without a soul." And forthwith he prayed with all his might that life should be breathed into it.

'And his prayer was heard: the beautiful statue became a living girl, and the three men all fell in love with her, and each desired to have her to wife.

'Now,' said the nightingale, 'to which of them did the maiden really belong? It seems to me that the carpenter had the best right to her.'

'Oh, but the student would never have thought of praying that she might be given a soul had not the tailor drawn attention to her loveliness by the robe which he put upon her,' answered the prince, who guessed what he was expected to say; and they soon set up quite a pretty quarrel. Suddenly the princess, furious that neither of them alluded to the part played by the student, quite forgot her vow of silence and cried loudly:

'Idiots that you are! How could she belong to any one but

the student? If it had not been for him, all that the others did would have gone for nothing! Of course it was he who married the maiden!' And as she spoke the seven veils fell from her, and she stood up, the fairest princess the world has ever seen.

'You have won me,' she said smiling, holding out her hand to the prince.

And so they were married; and after the wedding feast was over they sent for the old woman whose pitcher the prince had broken so long ago, and she dwelt in the palace, became nurse to their children, and lived happily till she died.

[Adapted from *Türkische Volksmärchen aus Stambul gesammelt, übersetzt und eingeleitet* von Dr. Ignaz Künos. Brilla, Leiden.]

Jackal or Tiger?

ONE HOT NIGHT, IN Hindustan, a king and queen lay awake in the palace in the midst of the city. Every now and then a faint air blew through the lattice, and they hoped they were going to sleep, but they never did. Presently they became more broad awake than ever at the sound of a howl outside the palace.

'Listen to that tiger!' remarked the king.

'Tiger?' replied the queen. 'How should there be a tiger inside the city? It was only a jackal.'

'I tell you it was a tiger,' said the king.

'And I tell you that you were dreaming if you thought it was anything but a jackal,' answered the queen.

'I say it was a tiger!' cried the king. 'Don't contradict me.'

'Nonsense!' snapped the queen. 'It was a jackal.'

The dispute waxed so warm that the king said at last, 'Very well, we'll call the guard and ask. If it was a jackal I'll leave this kingdom to you and go away, but if it was a tiger then you shall go and I will marry a new wife.'

'As you like,' answered the queen. 'There isn't any doubt which it was.'

So the king called the two soldiers who were on guard outside and put the question to them. But, while the dispute was going on, the king and queen had become so excited and talked so loud that the guards had heard nearly all they said, and one man observed to the other:

'Mind you declare that the king is right. It certainly was a jackal, but if we say so, the king will probably not keep his word about going away and we shall get into trouble, so we had better take his side.'

Therefore, when the king asked what animal they had seen, both the guards said it was certainly a tiger, and that the king was right of course, as he always was. The king made no remark, but sent for a palanquin, and ordered its four bearers to take the queen a long way off into the forest and there leave her. In spite of her tears, away the bearers went for three days and three nights until they came to a dense wood. There they set down the palanquin with the queen in it, and started home again.

Now the queen thought the king could not mean to send her away for good and that, as soon as he had got over his fit of temper, he would summon her back. She stayed quite still for a long time, listening with all her ears for approaching footsteps, but heard none. After a while she grew nervous, for she was all alone, and put her head out of the palanquin and looked about her. Day was just breaking and birds and insects were beginning to stir; the leaves rustled in a warm breeze; but although the queen's eyes wandered in all directions, there was no sign of any human being. Then her spirit gave way and she began to cry.

Close to the spot where the queen had been set down dwelt a man who had a tiny farm in the midst of the forest, far from any neighbors. As it was hot weather the farmer had been sleeping on the flat roof of his house, but was awakened

by the sound of weeping. He jumped up and ran into the forest, and there he found the palanquin.

'Oh, poor soul that weeps,' cried the farmer, standing a little
way off, 'who are you?' At this salutation from a stranger the
queen grew silent, dreading she knew not what.

'Oh, you that weep,' repeated the farmer, 'fear not to speak
to me, for you are to me as a daughter. Tell me, who are you?'

His voice was so kind that the queen gathered up her courage and spoke. When she had told her story, the farmer called
his wife, who led her to their house, and gave her food to eat
and a bed to lie on. And in the farm, a few days later, a
little prince was born, and by his mother's wish, named Ameer
Ali.

Years passed without a sign from the king. His wife might
have been dead for all he seemed to care. The little prince had
by this time grown up into a strong, handsome and healthy
youth. The prince was continually begging his mother and
the farmer to be allowed to go away and seek adventures and
to make his own living. But she and the wise farmer always
counseled him to wait, until at last, when he was eighteen
years of age, they had not the heart to forbid him any longer.
So he started off early one morning, with a sword by his side,
a big brass pot to hold water, a few pieces of silver and a galail,
or two-stringed bow, in his hand, with which to shoot birds
as he traveled.

Many a weary mile he tramped. As he made his way through
a thicket, he saw a pigeon which he thought would make a
good dinner. He fired a pellet at it from his galail, but missed
the pigeon which fluttered away. At the same instant he heard
a great clamor from beyond the thicket, and on reaching the
spot, he found an ugly old woman streaming wet and crying
loudly as she lifted from her head an earthen vessel with a

hole in it. When she saw the prince with his galail in his hand, she called out:

'Oh, wretched one! Why must you choose an old woman like me to play your pranks upon? Where am I to get a fresh pitcher instead of this one you have broken with your foolish tricks? And how am I to go so far for water twice when one journey wearies me?'

'But, mother,' replied the prince, 'I played no trick upon you! I did but shoot at a pigeon that should have served me for dinner. I missed, and my pellet must have broken your pitcher. But, in exchange, you shall have my brass pot; that will not break easily; and as for getting water, tell me where to find it and I'll fetch it, while you dry your garments in the sun, and carry it whither you will.'

At this the old woman's face brightened. She showed him where to seek the water, and when he returned a few minutes later with his pot filled to the brim, she led the way without a word and he followed. In a short while they came to a hut in the forest, and as they drew near it Ameer Ali beheld in the doorway the loveliest damsel his eyes had ever looked on.

At the sight of a stranger she drew her veil about her and stepped into the hut, and much as he wished to see her again, Ameer Ali could think of no excuse by which to bring her back and so, with a heavy heart, he made his salutation and bade the old woman farewell. But when he had gone a little way she called after him:

'If ever you are in trouble or danger, come to where you now stand, and cry, "Fairy of the Forest! Fairy of the Forest, help me now!" And I will listen to you.'

The prince thanked her and continued his journey, but he thought little of the old woman's saying and much of the lovely damsel. Shortly afterward he arrived at a city, and as he was now in great straits, having come to the end of his money, he walked to the palace and asked for employment.

The king said he had plenty of servants and wanted no more, but the young man pleaded so hard that at last the rajah was sorry for him and promised he should enter his bodyguard on the condition that he would undertake any service which was especially difficult or dangerous. This was just what Ameer Ali wanted, and he agreed to do whatever the king might wish.

Soon after this, on a dark and stormy night, when the river roared beneath the palace walls, the sound of a woman weeping and wailing was heard. The king ordered a servant to see what was the matter. But the servant, falling on his knees in terror, begged that he might not be sent on such an errand on a night so wild. Evil spirits and witches were sure to be abroad. Indeed, so frightened was he, that the king, who was very kind-hearted, bade another go in his stead, but each one showed the same strange fear. Then Ameer Ali stepped forward:

'This is my duty, Your Majesty,' he said. 'I will go.'

The king nodded, and off Ameer Ali went. The night was as dark as pitch, and the wind blew furiously and drove the rain in sheets into his face, but he made his way down to the ford under the palace walls and stepped into the flooded water. Inch by inch, and foot by foot, he fought his way across, now nearly swept off his feet by some sudden swirl or eddy, now narrowly escaping being caught in the branches of some floating tree that came tossing and swinging down the stream. At length he emerged, panting and dripping wet, on the other side. Close by the bank stood a gallows, and on the gallows hung the body of some evil-doer, while from the foot of it came the sound of sobbing that the king had heard.

Ameer Ali was so grieved for the one who wept that he thought nothing of the wildness of the night or of the roaring river. As for ghosts and witches, they had never troubled him, so he walked up toward the gallows where crouched the figure of the woman.

'What ails you?' he said.

Now the woman was not really a woman at all, but a horrid kind of witch, who really lived in Witchland, and had no business on earth. If ever a man strayed into Witchland the ogresses used to eat him up, and this old witch thought she would like to catch a man for supper, and that is why she had been sobbing and crying in hopes that someone out of pity might come to her rescue.

So when Ameer Ali questioned her, she replied, 'Ah, kind sir, it is my poor son who hangs upon that gallows. Help me to get him down and I will bless you forever.'

Ameer Ali thought her voice sounded rather more eager than sorrowful. He suspected she was not telling the truth, so he determined to be very cautious.

'That will be rather difficult,' he said, 'for the gallows is high, and we have no ladder.'

'Ah, but if you will just stoop down and let me climb upon your shoulders,' answered the old witch, 'I think I could reach him.' But her voice now sounded so cruel that Ameer Ali was sure she intended some evil, and he only said:

'Very well, we will try.' With that he drew his sword, pretending that he needed it to lean upon, and bent so that the old woman could clamber on to his back, which she did very nimbly. Then, suddenly, he felt a noose slipped over his neck, and the old witch sprang from his shoulders on to the gallows, crying:

'Now, foolish one, I have you and will kill you for my supper.'

But Ameer Ali gave a sweep upward with his sharp sword to cut the rope she had slipped round his neck, and not only cut the cord but cut also the old woman's foot as it dangled above him. And with a yell of pain and anger she vanished into the darkness.

Ameer Ali then sat down to collect himself a little, and felt upon the ground by his side an anklet that had evidently fallen off the old witch's foot. This he put into his pocket, and as the storm had by this time passed over he made his way back to the palace. When he had finished his story, he took the anklet out of his pocket and handed it to the king who, like everyone else, was amazed at the glory of the jewels which composed it. Indeed, Ameer Ali himself was astonished, for he had slipped the anklet into his pocket in the dark and had not looked at it since. The king was delighted with its beauty, and having praised and rewarded Ameer Ali, he gave the anklet to his daughter, a proud and spoiled princess.

Now in the women's apartments in the palace there hung two cages, in one of which was a parrot and in the other a starling, and these two birds could talk as well as human beings. They were both pets of the princess who always fed them herself, and the next day, as she was walking grandly about with her treasure round her ankle, she heard the starling say to the parrot:

'Oh, Toté, how do you think the princess looks in her new jewel?'

'Think?' snapped the parrot, who was cross because he hadn't had his bath that morning. 'I think she looks like a washerwoman's daughter, with one shoe on and the other off! Why doesn't she wear two of them, instead of going about with one leg adorned and the other bare?'

When the princess heard this she burst into tears, and sending for her father, she declared that he must get her another such anklet to wear, or she would die of shame. So the king sent for Ameer Ali and told him he must get a second anklet exactly like the first within a month, or he should be hanged.

Poor Ameer Ali was greatly troubled at the king's command. He left the palace at once and inquired of everyone where the finest jewels were to be had, but though he sought night and day he never found one to compare with the anklet. At last only a week remained, and he was in sore difficulty, when he remembered the Fairy of the Forest and determined to go without loss of time to seek her. Therefore, away he went, and after a day's traveling he reached the cottage in the forest, and standing where he had stood when the old woman called to him, he cried:

'Fairy of the Forest! Fairy of the Forest! Help me! Help me!'

Then in the doorway appeared the beautiful girl he had seen before, whom in all his wanderings he had never forgotten.

'What is the matter?' she asked, in a voice so soft that he listened like one struck dumb, and she had to repeat the question before he could answer. Then he told her his story, and she went within the cottage and came back with two wands and a pot of boiling water. The two wands she planted in the ground about six feet apart, and then turning to him, she said:

'I am going to lie down between these two wands. You must then draw your sword and cut off my foot, and as soon as you have done that, you must seize it and hold it over the caldron, and every drop of blood that falls from it into the water will become a jewel. Next you must change the wands so the one that stood at my head is at my feet, and the one at my feet stands at my head, and place the severed foot against the wound and it will heal, and I shall become quite well again as before.'

At first Ameer Ali declared that he would sooner be hanged twenty times over than treat her so roughly, but at length she persuaded him to do her bidding. He nearly fainted with horror when he found that, after the cruel blow which lopped off her foot, she lay as one lifeless. But he held the severed foot over the caldron, and as drops of blood fell from it and he saw each turn into a shining gem, his heart took courage. Very soon there were plenty of jewels in the caldron and he quickly changed the wands, placed the severed foot against the wound, and immediately the two parts became one as before.

Then the maiden opened her eyes, sprang to her feet and, drawing her veil about her, ran into the hut and would not come out or speak to him any more. For a long while he waited

In the doorway appeared the beautiful girl

but, as she did not appear, he gathered up the precious stones and returned to the palace. He easily found someone to set the jewels, and found there were enough to make, not only one, but three rare and beautiful anklets, and these he duly presented to the king on the very day that his month of grace was over.

The king embraced him warmly and made him rich gifts, and the next day the vain princess put two anklets on each foot, and strutted up and down in them, admiring herself in the mirrors that lined her room.

'Oh, Toté,' asked the starling, 'how do you think our princess looks now in these fine jewels?'

'Ugh,' growled the parrot, who was always cross in the mornings and never recovered his temper until after lunch, 'she's got all her beauty at one end of her now. If she had a few of those fine gewgaws round her neck and wrists she would look better; but now, to my mind, she looks more than ever like the washerwoman's daughter dressed up.'

Poor princess! She wept and stormed and raved until she made herself quite ill, and then she declared to her father that, unless she had bracelets and a necklace to match the anklets, she would die.

Again the king sent for Ameer Ali and ordered him to get a necklace and bracelets to match those anklets within a month or be put to a cruel death.

Again Ameer Ali spent nearly the whole month searching for the jewels, but all in vain. At length he made his way to the hut in the forest, and cried:

'Fairy of the Forest! Fairy of the Forest! Help me! Help me!'

Once more the beautiful maiden appeared at his summons

and asked what he wanted, and when he had told her she said he must do exactly as he had done the first time, except that now he must cut off both her hands and her head. Her words turned Ameer Ali pale with horror; but she reminded him that no harm had come to her before, and at last he consented to do as she bade him.

From her severed hands and head there fell into the caldron bracelets and chains of rubies and diamonds, emeralds and pearls that surpassed any that ever were seen. Then the head and hands were joined again to the body and left neither sign nor scar. Full of gratitude, Ameer Ali tried to speak to her, but she ran into the house and would not come back, and he was forced to leave her and go away laden with the jewels.

When, on the day appointed, Ameer Ali produced a necklace and bracelets, each more beautiful and priceless than the last, the king's astonishment knew no bounds, and as for his daughter she was nearly mad with joy. The very next morning she put on all her finery and thought that now, at least, that disagreeable parrot could find no fault with her appearance, and she listened eagerly when she heard the starling say:

'Oh, Toté, how do you think our princess is looking now?'

'Very fine, no doubt,' grumbled the parrot, 'but what is the use of dressing up like that for oneself only? She ought to have a husband. Why doesn't she marry the man who brought her all these splendid things?'

Then the princess went to her father and told him that she wished to marry Ameer Ali.

'My dear child,' said her father, 'you really are very difficult to please and want something new every day. It certainly is time you married someone. If you choose this man, of course he shall marry you.'

So the king sent for Ameer Ali and told him that, within a month, he proposed to do him the honor of marrying him to the princess and making him heir to the throne.

On hearing this speech Ameer Ali bowed low and answered that he had done and would do the king all the service that lay in his power, save only this one thing. The king, who considered his daughter's hand a prize for any man, flew into a passion, and the princess was more furious still. Ameer Ali was instantly thrown into the most dismal prison they could find, to be kept there until the king had time to think in what way he should be put to death.

Meanwhile the king determined that the princess should in any case be married without delay, so he sent forth heralds throughout the neighboring countries, proclaiming that on a certain day any person, fitted for a bridegroom and heir to the throne, should present himself at the palace.

When the day came, all the court gathered together, and a great crowd of men assembled, young and old, who thought they had as good a chance as anyone else to gain both the throne and the princess. As soon as the king was seated, he called upon an usher to summon the first claimant. But, just then, a farmer who stood in front of the crowd cried out that he had a petition to offer.

'Well, hasten then,' said the king. 'I have no time to waste.'

'Your Majesty,' said the farmer, 'has now lived and administered justice long in this city and will know that the tiger who is king of beasts hunts only in the forest, while jackals hunt in every place where there is something to be picked up.'

'What is all this? What is all this?' asked the king. 'The man must be mad!'

'No,' answered the farmer, 'I would only remind Your Majesty that plenty of jackals are gathered today to try and claim your daughter and kingdom: every city has sent them, and they wait hungry and eager; but do not, O King, mistake or pretend again to mistake the howl of a jackal for the hunting cry of a tiger.'

The king turned first red and then pale.

'There is,' continued the farmer, 'a royal tiger bred in the forest who has the first and only true claim to your throne.'

'Where? What do you mean?' stammered the king, growing pale as he listened.

'In prison,' replied the farmer. 'If Your Majesty will clear this court of the jackals I will explain.'

'Clear the court!' commanded the king. And very unwillingly the visitors left the palace.

'Now tell me what riddle this is,' said he.

Then the farmer told the king and his ministers how he had rescued the queen and brought up Ameer Ali, and he fetched the old queen herself, whom he had left outside. At the sight of her the king was filled with shame and self-reproach and wished he could have lived his life over again and not have married the mother of the proud princess who had caused him endless trouble until her death.

'My day is past,' said he. And he gave up his crown to his son, Ameer Ali, who went once more and called to the forest fairy to provide him with a queen to share his throne.

'There is only one person I will marry,' said he. And this time the maiden did not run away, but agreed to be his wife. So the two were married without delay and lived long and reigned happily.

As for the old woman whose pitcher Ameer Ali had broken, she was the forest maiden's fairy godmother, and when she was no longer needed to look after the girl she gladly returned to Fairyland.

The old king was never heard to contradict his wife any more. If he even looked as if he did not agree with her, she smiled at him and said:

'Is it the tiger, then, or the jackal?'

And he had not another word to say.

Moti

ONCE UPON A TIME there was a youth called Moti, who was very big and strong, but the clumsiest creature imaginable. So clumsy was he that he was always putting his great feet into the bowls of sweet milk or curds, which his mother set out on the floor to cool, always smashing, upsetting, breaking, until at last his father said to him:

'Here, Moti, are fifty silver pieces which are the savings of years. Take them and go and make your living or your fortune if you can.'

Then Moti started off one early spring morning, with his thick staff over his shoulder, singing gaily to himself as he walked along.

In one way and another he got along very well until a hot evening when he came to a certain city where he entered the travelers' serai, or inn, to pass the night. Now a serai is generally just a large square enclosed by a high wall, with an open colonnade along the inside all round to accommodate both men and beasts, and with perhaps a few rooms in towers at the corners for those who are too rich or too proud to care about sleeping by their own camels and horses.

Moti, of course, was a country lad and had lived with cattle all his life. He was neither rich nor proud, so he just borrowed a bed from the innkeeper, set it down beside an old buffalo who reminded him of home, and in five minutes was fast asleep.

In the middle of the night he woke, feeling that he had been disturbed and, putting his hand under his pillow, found to his horror that his bag of money had been stolen. He jumped up quietly and began to prowl around to see whether anyone seemed to be awake, but though he managed to arouse a few men and beasts by falling over them, he walked in the shadow of the archways round the whole serai without coming across a likely thief. He was just about to give it up when he over-heard two men whispering and one laughed softly. Peering behind a pillar, he saw two Afghan horse-dealers counting out his bag of money. Then Moti went back to bed!

In the morning Moti followed the two Afghans outside the city to the horse market in which their horses were offered for sale. Choosing the best-looking horse amongst them he went up to it and said, 'Is this horse for sale? May I try it?'

The merchants assenting, Moti scrambled up on its back, dug in his heels and off they flew. Now Moti had never been on a horse in his life and had so much ado to hold on with both hands as well as with both legs that the animal went just where it liked. Very soon it broke into a break-neck gallop and made straight back to the serai where it had spent the last few nights.

This will do very well, thought Moti as they whirled in at the entrance. As soon as the horse had arrived at its stable it stopped of its own accord and Moti immediately rolled off. But he jumped up at once, tied the beast up, and called for some breakfast. Presently the Afghans appeared, out of breath and furious, and claimed the horse.

'What do you mean?' cried Moti, with his mouth full of rice. 'It's my horse; I paid you fifty pieces of silver for it—quite a bargain, I'm sure!'

'Nonsense! It is our horse,' answered one of the Afghans, beginning to untie the bridle.

'Leave off!' shouted Moti, seizing his staff. 'If you don't let my horse alone I'll crack your skulls! You thieves! I know you! Last night you took my money, so today I took your horse. That's fair enough!'

Now the Afghans began to look a little uncomfortable. Moti seemed so determined they resolved to appeal to the law, so they went off and laid a complaint before the king that Moti had stolen one of their horses and would not give it up nor pay for it.

Presently a soldier came to summon Moti to the king. When he arrived and made his obeisance, the king began to question him as to why he had galloped off with the horse in this fashion. But Moti declared he had taken the animal in exchange for fifty pieces of silver, while the horse merchants vowed that the money they had on them was what they had received for the sale of other horses. In one way and another the dispute got so confusing that the king, who really thought Moti had stolen the horse, said at last, 'Well, I tell you what I will do. I will lock something into this box before me; if he guesses what it is, the horse is his, and if he doesn't, then it is yours.'

To this Moti agreed, and the king rose and went out alone by a little door at the back of the court. Presently he came back, clasping something closely wrapped up in a cloth under his robe, slipped it into the little box, locked the box, and set it up where all might see.

'Now,' said the king to Moti, 'guess!'

It happened that when the king had opened the door behind him, Moti noticed there was a garden outside. Watching for the king's return he began to wonder what could be had out of the garden small enough to be shut in the box.

'Is it likely to be a fruit or a flower? No, not a flower this time, for he clasped it too tight. Then it must be a fruit or a stone. Yet not a stone, because he wouldn't wrap a dirty stone in his nice clean cloth. Then it is a fruit! And a fruit without much scent, else he would be afraid I might smell it. Now what fruit without much scent is in season just now? When I know that I shall have guessed the riddle!'

As has been said before, Moti was a country lad and was accustomed to work in his father's garden. He knew all the common fruits, so he thought he should be able to guess right. Not to let it seem too easy, he gazed up at the ceiling with a puzzled expression, and looked down at the floor with an air of wisdom, his fingers pressed against his forehead. Then he said slowly, with his eyes on the king:

'It is freshly plucked! It is round and it is red! It is a pomegranate!'

Now the king knew nothing about fruits except that they were good to eat. As for seasons, he asked for whatever fruit he wanted, whenever he wanted it, and saw that he got it. To him Moti's guess was like a miracle and clear proof not only of his wisdom but of his innocence, for it was a pomegranate that he had put into the box. Of course, when the king marveled and praised Moti's wisdom, everybody else did so too, and while the Afghans went off crestfallen, Moti took the horse and entered the king's service.

Moti dragged the tiger back to the serai

Very soon after this, Moti, who continued to live in the serai, came back one wet and stormy evening to find that his precious horse had strayed. Nothing remained but a broken halter cord, and no one knew what had become of him. After inquiring of everyone who was likely to know, Moti seized the cord and his big staff and sallied out to look for him. Away and away he tramped, out of the city and into the neighboring forest, tracking hoofmarks in the mud. Presently it grew late, but still Moti wandered on until suddenly in the gathering darkness he came right upon a tiger who was contentedly eating his horse.

'You thief!' shrieked Moti. And just as the tiger, in astonishment, dropped a bone—whack! Down came Moti's staff on his head with such good will that the beast was half stunned and could hardly breathe or see. Then Moti continued to shower upon him blows and abuse until the poor tiger could hardly stand, whereupon his tormentor tied the end of the broken halter round his neck and dragged him back to the serai.

'If you had my horse,' he said, 'I will at least have you, that's fair enough!' And he tied the tiger up securely by the head and heels, much as he used to tie the horse. Then, the night being far gone, he flung himself down and slept soundly.

Just try to imagine anything like the fright of the people in the serai, when they woke up and found a tiger—very battered but still a tiger—securely tethered amongst themselves and their beasts! Men gathered in groups, talking and exclaiming, and finding fault with the innkeeper for allowing such a dangerous beast into the serai. All the while the innkeeper was just as troubled as the rest, and none dared go near the place where the tiger stood blinking miserably on everyone, and where Moti lay stretched out snoring like thunder.

At last news reached the king that Moti had exchanged his horse for a live tiger, and the monarch himself came down, half disbelieving the tale, to see if it were really true. Someone at last awoke Moti with the news that his royal master was come, and he arose, yawning, and was soon delightedly explaining and showing off his new possession.

The king, however, did not share his pleasure at all, but called up a soldier to shoot the tiger, much to the relief of all the inmates of the serai except Moti. If the king was convinced before that Moti was one of the wisest of men, he was now still more convinced that he was the bravest, and he increased his pay a hundredfold, and our hero thought that he was the luckiest of men.

A week or two after this incident the king sent for Moti who, on arrival, found his master in despair. A neighboring monarch, he explained, who had many more soldiers than he, had declared war against him, and he was at his wits' end, for he had neither money to buy him off nor soldiers enough to fight him—what was he to do?

'If that is all, don't you trouble,' said Moti. 'Turn out your men; I'll go with them and we'll soon bring this robber to reason.'

The king began to revive at these hopeful words and took Moti off to his stable, where he bade him choose for himself any horse he liked. There were plenty of fine horses in the stalls, but to the king's astonishment Moti chose a poor little pony that was used to carry grass and water for the rest of the stable.

'But why do you choose that beast?' asked the king.

'Well, you see, Your Majesty,' replied Moti, 'there are so many chances that I may fall off. If I choose one of your fine big horses I shall have so far to fall that I shall probably break my leg or my arm, if not my neck, but if I fall off this little beast I can't hurt myself much.'

A very comical sight was Moti when he rode out to the war. The only weapon he carried was his staff, and to help him to keep his balance on horseback he had tied to each of his ankles a big stone that nearly touched the ground as he sat astride the little pony. The rest of the king's cavalry were not very numerous, but they pranced along in armor on fine horses. Behind them came a great rabble of men on foot, armed with all sorts of weapons, and last of all was the king with his attendants, very nervous and ill at ease. So the army started.

They had not very far to go, but Moti's little pony, weighted with a heavy man and two big rocks, soon began to lag behind the cavalry and would have lagged behind the infantry too, only they were not very anxious to be too early in the fight and hung back to give Moti plenty of time. The young man jogged along more and more slowly for some time, until at last, getting impatient at the slowness of the pony, he gave him such a tremendous thwack with his staff that the pony completely lost his temper and bolted.

First one stone became untied and rolled away in a cloud of dust to one side of the road, while Moti nearly rolled off too, but clasped his steed valiantly by its ragged mane and, dropping his staff, held on for dear life. Then, fortunately, the other rock broke away from his other leg and rolled thunderously down a neighboring ravine. Meanwhile the advanced cavalry had barely time to draw to one side when Moti came dashing by, yelling bloodthirsty threats to his pony:

'You wait till I get hold of you! I'll skin you alive! I'll wring your neck! I'll break every bone in your body!'

The cavalry thought that this dreadful language was meant for the enemy and were filled with admiration of his courage.

Many of their horses too were quite upset by this whirlwind that galloped howling through their midst, and in a few minutes, after a little plunging and rearing and kicking, the whole troop were following on Moti's heels.

Far in advance, Moti continued his wild career. Presently in his course he came to a great field of castor-oil plants, ten or twelve feet high, big and bushy, but quite green and soft. Hoping to escape from the back of his fiery steed Moti grasped one in passing, but its roots gave way, and he dashed on, with the whole plant looking like a young tree flourishing in his grip.

The enemy were in battle array, advancing over the plain, their king with them confident and cheerful, when suddenly from the front came a desperate rider at a furious gallop.

'Sire!' he cried. 'Save yourself! The enemy are coming!'

'What do you mean?' said the king.

'Oh, sire,' panted the messenger, 'fly at once, there is no time to lose! Foremost of the enemy rides a mad giant at a furious gallop. He flourishes a tree for a club and is wild with anger, for as he goes he cries, "You wait till I get hold of you! I'll skin you alive! I'll wring your neck! I'll break every bone in your body!" Others ride behind, and you will do well to retire before this whirlwind of destruction comes upon you.'

Just then out of a cloud of dust in the distance the king saw Moti approaching at a hard gallop, looking indeed like a giant compared with the little beast he rode, whirling his caster-oil plant, which in the distance might have been an oak tree, and the sound of his revilings and shoutings came down upon the breeze! Behind him the dust cloud moved to the sound of the thunder of hoofs, while here and there flashed the glitter of steel. The sight and the sound struck terror into the king, and turning his horse, he fled at top speed, thinking that a regiment of yelling giants was upon him, and all his force followed him as fast as they might go.

One fat officer alone could not keep up on foot with that mad rush, and as Moti came galloping up he flung himself on the ground in abject fear. This was too much for Moti's excited pony who shied so suddenly that Moti went flying over his head like a skyrocket and alighted right on top of his fat foe.

Quickly regaining his feet Moti began to swing his plant round his head and to shout, 'Where are your men? Bring them up and I'll kill them. My regiments! Come on, the whole lot of you! Where's your king? Bring him to me. Here are all my fine fellows coming up and we'll each pull up a tree by the roots and lay you all flat and your houses and towns and everything else! Come on!'

But the poor fat officer could do nothing but squat on his knees with his hands together, gasping. At last, when he caught his breath, Moti sent him off to bring his king and to tell him that if he was reasonable his life should be spared.

Off the poor man went, and by the time the troops of Moti's side had come up and arranged themselves to look as formidable as possible, he returned with his king. The latter was very humble and apologetic and promised never to make war any more, to pay a large sum of money, and altogether do whatever his conqueror wished.

So the armies on both sides went rejoicing home, and this was really the making of the fortune of clumsy Moti who lived long and contrived always to be looked up to as a fountain of wisdom, valor and discretion by all except his relations. They could never understand what he had done to be considered so much wiser than anyone else.

[A Pushto Story.]

Kupti and Imani

NCE THERE WAS A
king who had two daughters and their names were Kupti and
Imani. He loved them both very much and spent hours in
talking to them. One day he said to Kupti, the elder:

'Are you satisfied to leave your life and fortune in my
hands?'

'Verily, yes,' answered the princess, surprised at the question. 'In whose hands should I leave them, if not in yours?'

But when he asked his younger daughter Imani the same
question, she replied:

'No, indeed! If I had the chance I would make my own
fortune.'

At this answer the king was very displeased, and said, 'You
are too young to know the meaning of your words. But, be it
so, my daughter, I will give you the chance of gratifying
your wish.'

Then he sent for an old lame fakir who lived in a tumble-
down hut on the outskirts of the city, and when he had presented himself, the king said:

'No doubt, as you are very old and nearly crippled, you
would be glad to have some young person live with you and

serve you; so I will send you my younger daughter. She wants to earn her living and she can do so with you.'

Of course the old fakir had not a word to say, or if he had, he was really too astonished and troubled to say it. But the young princess went off with him smiling, and tripped along quite gaily, while he hobbled home with her in perplexed silence.

Directly they reached the hut the fakir began to think what he could arrange for the princess' comfort. But after all he was a fakir, and his house was bare except for one bedstead, two old cooking pots and an earthen jar for water, and one cannot get much comfort out of such things. However, the princess soon ended his perplexity by asking:

'Have you any money?'

'I have a penny somewhere,' replied the fakir.

'Very well,' rejoined the princess, 'give me the penny and go out and borrow me a spinning wheel and a loom.'

After much seeking the fakir found the penny and started on his errand, while the princess went shopping. First she bought a farthing's worth of oil, and then she bought three farthings' worth of flax. When she returned with her purchases she set the old man on the bedstead and rubbed his crippled leg with the oil for an hour.

Then she sat down to the spinning wheel and spun and spun all night long while the old man slept. In the morning, she had spun the finest thread that ever was seen. Next she went to the loom and wove and wove until by the evening she had woven a beautiful silver cloth.

'Now,' said she to the fakir, 'go into the market place and sell my cloth while I rest.'

'And what am I to ask for it?' said the old man.

'Two gold pieces,' replied the princess.

So the fakir hobbled away, and stood in the market place to sell the cloth. Presently the elder princess drove by, and when she saw the cloth she stopped and asked the price, for it was better work than she or any of her women could weave.

'Two gold pieces,' said the fakir. And the princess gladly paid them, after which the old fakir hobbled home with the money.

As she had done before so Imani did again day after day. Always she spent a penny upon oil and flax, always she tended the old man's lame leg, and spun and wove the most beautiful cloths and sold them at high prices. Gradually the city became famous for her beautiful stuffs, the old fakir's lame leg became straighter and stronger, and the hole under the floor of the hut where they kept their money became fuller and fuller of gold pieces. At last, one day, the princess said:

'I really think we have enough to live on in greater comfort.' She sent for builders, and they built a beautiful house for her and the old fakir, and in all the city there was none finer except the king's palace. Presently this reached the ears of the king, and when he inquired whose it was they told him that it belonged to his daughter.

'Well,' exclaimed the king, 'she said that she would make her own fortune, and somehow or other she seems to have done it!'

A little while after this, business took the king to another country, and before he went he asked his elder daughter what she would like him to bring her back as a gift.

'A necklace of rubies,' answered she. And then the king thought he would like to ask Imani too; so he sent a messenger to find out what sort of present she wanted. The man happened to arrive just as she was trying to disentangle a knot in her loom, and bowing low before her, he said:

'The king sends me to inquire what you wish him to bring you as a present from the country of Dûr?' But Imani, who was only considering how she could best untie the knot without breaking the thread, replied:

'Patience,' meaning that the messenger should wait till she was able to attend to him. But the messenger went off with this as an answer and told the king that the only thing Princess Imani wanted was patience.

'Oh!' said the king. 'I don't know whether that's a thing to be bought at Dûr. I never had it myself, but if it is to be found I will buy it for her.'

Next day the king departed on his journey, and when his business at Dûr was completed he bought for Kupti a beautiful ruby necklace. Then he said to a servant:

'The Princess Imani wants some patience. I did not know there was such a thing, but you must go to the market and inquire, and if any is to be sold, get it and bring it to me.'

The servant saluted and left the king's presence. He walked about the market for some time crying, 'Has anyone patience to sell? Patience to sell?' And some of the people mocked, and some, who had no patience, told him to go away and not be a fool, and some said, 'The fellow's mad! As though one could buy or sell patience!'

At length it came to the ears of the King of Dûr that a mad-man was in the market trying to buy patience. The king laughed and said:

'I should like to see that fellow, bring him here!'

And immediately his attendants went to seek the man and brought him to the king, who asked, 'What is this you want?'

And the man replied, 'Sire, I am bidden to ask for patience.'

'Oh,' said the king, 'you must have a strange master! What does he want with it?'

'My master wants it as a present for his daughter Imani,' replied the servant.

'Well,' said the king, 'I know of some patience which the young lady might have if she cares for it, but it is not to be bought.'

Now the king's name was Subbar Khan, and Subbar means patience; but the messenger did not know that, or understand that he was making a joke. However, he declared that Prin-cess Imani was not only young and beautiful, but also the cleverest, most industrious and kindest-hearted of princesses. And he would have gone on explaining her virtues had not the king laughingly put up his hand and stopped him, say-ing: 'Well, well, wait a minute, and I will see what can be done.'

With that he rose and went to his own apartments and took out a little casket. Into the casket he put a fan, and shut-ting it up carefully, he brought it to the messenger and said:

'Here is a casket. It has neither lock nor key and yet will open only to the touch of the person who needs its contents—

The princess summoned the king with a wave of her fan

and whoever opens it will obtain patience; but I cannot tell whether it will be the kind of patience that is wanted.'

The servant bowed low and took the casket, but when he asked what was to be paid, the king would take nothing. So he went away and gave the casket and an account of his adventures to his master.

As soon as their father returned to his country, Kupti and Imani each received the presents he had brought for them. Imani was very surprised when the casket was brought to her by the hand of a messenger.

'But,' she said, 'what is this? I never asked for anything! Indeed I had no time, for the messenger ran away before I had unraveled my tangle.'

But the servant declared the casket was for her, so she took it with some curiosity and brought it to the old fakir. The old man tried to open it, but in vain—so closely did the lid fit that it seemed to be quite immovable, and yet there was neither lock nor bolt nor spring, nor anything apparently by which the casket was kept shut. When he was tired of trying he handed the casket to the princess, who hardly touched it before it opened quite easily, and there lay within a beautiful fan. With a cry of surprise and pleasure Imani took out the fan and began to fan herself.

Hardly had she finished three strokes of the fan before there suddenly appeared before her King Subbar Khan of Dûr! The princess gasped and rubbed her eyes, and the old fakir sat and gazed in such astonishment that for some minutes he could not speak. At length he said:

'Who may you be, fair sir, if you please?'

'My name,' said the king, 'is Subbar Khan of Dûr. This lady,' bowing to the princess, 'has summoned me, and here I am!'

'I?' stammered the princess. 'I have summoned you? I never saw or heard of you in my life before, so how could that be?'

Then the king told them how he had heard of a man in his own city of Dûr trying to buy patience, and how he had given him the fan in the casket. 'Both are magical,' he added. 'When anyone uses the fan, in three strokes of it I am with her; if she folds it and taps it on the table, in three taps I am at home again. The casket will not open to all, but you see it was this fair lady who asked for patience, and as that is my name, here I am, very much at her service.'

Now Princess Imani, being of a high spirit, was anxious to fold up the fan and give the three taps which would send the king home again. But the old fakir was very pleased with his guest, and so in one way and another they spent a pleasant evening together before Subbar Khan took his leave.

After that he was often summoned, and as both the fakir and he were very fond of chess and were good players, they used to sit up half the night playing, and at last a little room in the house began to be called the king's room. Whenever he stayed late he used to sleep there and go home again in the morning.

By-and-by it came to the ears of Princess Kupti that a rich and handsome young man was visiting at her sister's house, and she was very jealous. So she went one day to pay Imani a visit, pretending to be very affectionate and interested in the house, and in the way in which Imani and the old fakir lived, and of their mysterious and royal visitor.

As the sisters went from place to place, Kupti was shown Subbar Khan's room; and presently, making some excuse, she slipped in by herself and swiftly spread under the sheet which lay upon the bed a quantity of very finely powdered and splintered glass which was poisoned, and which she had brought with her concealed in her clothes. Shortly afterward she took leave of her sister, declaring she could never forgive herself for not having come near her all this time, and that she would now begin to make amends for her neglect.

That very evening Subbar Khan came and sat up late with the old fakir playing chess as usual. Very tired, he at length bade him and the princess good night and, as soon as he lay down on the bed, thousands of tiny, tiny splinters of poisoned glass ran into him. He could not think what was the matter, and turned this way and that until he was pricked all over and felt as though he were burning from head to foot. But he said never a word, only sitting up all night in agony of body and in worse agony of mind to think that he should have been poisoned, as he guessed he was, in Imani's own house.

In the morning, although he was nearly fainting, he still said nothing, and by means of the magic fan was duly transported home again. Then he sent for all the physicians and doctors in his kingdom, but none could make out what his illness was. And so he lingered on for weeks and weeks, trying every remedy that anyone could devise, and passing sleepless nights and days of pain and fever and misery, until at last he was at the point of death.

Meanwhile Princess Imani and the old fakir were much troubled because, although they waved the magic fan again and again, no Subbar Khan appeared, and they feared that he had tired of them, or that some evil fate had overtaken him. At last the princess was in such a miserable state of doubt and uncertainty that she determined to go herself to the kingdom of Dûr and see what was the matter. Disguising herself as a young fakir, she set out upon her journey alone and on foot, as a fakir should travel.

One evening she found herself in a forest and lay down

under a great tree to pass the night. But she could not sleep
for thinking of Subbar Khan and wondering what had happened to him. Presently she heard two great monkeys talking to
one another in the tree above her head.

'Good evening, brother,' said one, 'whence come you and
what is the news?'

'I come from Dûr,' said the other, 'and the news is that the
king is dying.'

'Oh,' said the first, 'I'm sorry to hear that, for he is a master
hand at slaying leopards and creatures that ought not to be
allowed to live. What is the matter with him?'

'No man knows,' replied the second monkey, 'but the birds,
who see all and carry all messages, say that he is dying of
poisoned glass that Kupti the king's daughter spread upon his
bed.'

'Ah,' said the first monkey, 'that is sad news. But if they
only knew it, the berries of the very tree we sit in, steeped in
hot water, will cure such a disease as that in three days at most.'

'True!' said the other. 'It is a pity we cannot tell some man
of a medicine so simple and so save a good man's life. But
men are so silly; they go and shut themselves up in stuffy
houses in stuffy cities instead of living in nice airy trees, and
so they miss knowing all the best things.'

Now when Imani heard that Subbar Khan was dying she
began to weep silently, but as she listened she dried her tears
and sat up, and as soon as daylight dawned over the forest she
began to gather the berries from the tree until she had filled
her cloth with a load of them. Then she walked on as fast as
she could, and in two days reached the city of Dûr. The first
thing she did was to pass through the market crying:

'Medicine for sale! Are any ill that need my medicine?'

And presently one man said to his neighbor, 'See, there is

a young fakir with medicine for sale, perhaps he could do something for the king.'

'Pooh,' replied the other, 'where so many graybeards have failed, how should a lad like that be of any use?'

'Still,' said the first, 'he might try.' And he went up and spoke to Imani, and together they set out for the palace and announced that another doctor was come to try and cure the king.

After some delay Imani was admitted to the sick room, and, while she was so well disguised that the king did not recognize her, he was so wasted by illness that she hardly knew him. But she began at once, full of hope, by asking for some apartment all to herself and a pot in which to boil water.

As soon as the water was heated she steeped some of her berries in it and, giving the mixture to the king's attendants, told them to wash his body with it. The first washing did so much good that the king slept quietly all the night. Again the second day she did the same, and this time the king declared he was hungry and called for food. After the third day he was quite well, only very weak from his long illness. On the fourth day he got up and sat upon his throne, and then sent messengers to fetch the physician who had cured him.

When Imani appeared everyone marveled that so young a man should be so clever a doctor, and the king wanted to give him immense presents of money and of all kinds of precious things. At first Imani would take nothing, but at last she said that, if she must be rewarded, she would ask for the king's signet ring and his handkerchief. So, as she would take nothing more, the king gave her his signet ring and his handkerchief, and she departed and traveled back to her own country as fast as she could.

A little while after her return, when she had related to the fakir all her adventures, they sent for Subbar Khan by means of the magic fan, and when he appeared they asked him why he had stayed away for so long. Then he told them all about his illness, and how he had been cured, and when he had finished, the princess rose up and, opening a cabinet, brought out the ring and handkerchief, and said, laughing:

'Are these the rewards you gave to your doctor?'

At that the king recognized her and understood in a moment all that had happened, and he jumped up and put the magic fan in his pocket, declaring that no one should send him away to his own country any more unless Imani would come with him and be his wife. And so it was settled, and the old fakir and Imani went to the city of Dûr, where Imani was married to the king and lived happily ever after.

[Punjâbi story.]

Wali Dâd the Simple-hearted

ONCE UPON A TIME
there lived a poor old man whose name was Wali Dâd Gunjay,
or Wali Dâd the Bald. He had no relations, but lived all by
himself in a little mud hut some distance from any town, and
made his living by cutting grass in the jungle and selling it
as fodder for horses. He only earned by this five halfpence a
day, but he was a simple old man, and needed so little out of
it that he saved up one halfpenny daily, and spent the rest
upon such food and clothing as he required.

In this way he lived for many years until, one night, he
thought he would count the money he had hidden away in
the great earthen pot under the floor of his hut. So with much
trouble he pulled the bag out on to the floor and sat gazing in
astonishment at the heap of coins which tumbled out of it.

What should he do with them all? he wondered. But he
never thought of spending the money on himself, because he
was content to pass the rest of his days as he had been doing
for ever so long, and he really had no desire for any greater
comfort or luxury. At last he threw all the money into an old
sack, which he pushed under his bed, and then, rolled in his
ragged old blanket, went to sleep.

Early next morning he staggered off with his sack of money to the shop of a jeweler he knew in the town, and bargained with him for a beautiful little gold bracelet. With this carefully wrapped up in his cotton waistband he went to the house of a rich friend, who was a traveling merchant and used to wander about with his camels and merchandise through many countries. Wali Dâd was lucky enough to find him at home, so he sat down, and after a little talk he asked the merchant who was the most virtuous and beautiful lady he had ever met. The merchant replied that the Princess of Khaistân was renowned everywhere as well for the beauty of her person as for the kindness and generosity of her disposition.

'Then,' said Wali Dâd, 'next time you go that way, give her this little bracelet, with the respectful compliments of one who admires virtue far more than he desires wealth.'

With that he pulled the bracelet from his waistband and handed it to his friend. The merchant was naturally much astonished, but made no objection to carrying out his friend's plan.

Time passed by, and at length the merchant arrived in the course of his travels at the capital of Khaistân. As soon as he had opportunity he presented himself at the palace and sent in the bracelet, neatly packed in a little perfumed box provided by himself, giving at the same time the message entrusted to him by Wali Dâd.

The princess could not think who could have bestowed this present on her, but she bade her servant tell the merchant that if he would return, after he had finished his business in the city, she would give him her reply. In a few days, therefore, the merchant came back and received from the princess a return present in the shape of a camel-load of rich silks, besides a present of money for himself. With these he set out on his journey.

Some months later he was home again from his journeyings and proceeded to take Wali Dâd the princess' present. Great was the perplexity of the good man to find a camel-load of silks tumbled at his door! What was he to do with these costly things? But, presently, after much thought, he begged the merchant to consider whether he did not know of some young prince to whom such treasures might be useful.

'Of course,' cried the merchant, greatly amused, 'from Delhi to Baghdad, and from Constantinople to Lucknow, I know them all; and there lives none worthier than the gallant and wealthy young Prince of Nekabad.'

'Very well, then, take the silks to him, with the blessing of an old man,' said Wali Dâd, much relieved to be rid of them.

So the next time the merchant journeyed that way he carried the silks with him, and in due course arrived at Nekabad and sought an audience of the prince. When he was shown into his presence he produced the beautiful gift of silks that Wali Dâd had sent, and begged the young man to accept them as a humble tribute to his worth and greatness. The prince was much touched by the generosity of the giver and ordered, as a return present, twelve of the finest breed of horses for which his country was famous to be delivered over to the merchant, to whom also, before he took his leave, he gave a munificent reward for his services.

As before, the merchant at last arrived at home, and next day, he set out for Wali Dâd's house with the twelve horses. When the old man saw them coming in the distance he said to himself:

'Here's luck! A troop of horses coming! They are sure to want quantities of grass, and I shall sell all I have without having to drag it to market.' Thereupon he rushed off and cut grass as fast as he could.

When he came back, with as much grass as he could possibly carry, he was greatly discomfited to find that the horses were all for himself. At first he could not think what to do with them, but after a little, a brilliant idea struck him! He gave two to the merchant, and begged him to take the rest to the Princess of Khaistân, who was clearly the fittest person to possess such beautiful animals.

The merchant departed, laughing. But, true to his old friend's request, he took the horses with him on his next journey and eventually presented them safely to the princess. This time the princess sent for the merchant and questioned him about the giver. Now, the merchant was usually a most honest man, but he did not quite like to describe Wali Dâd in his true light as an old man whose income was five halfpence a day, and who had hardly clothes to cover him. So he told her that his friend had heard stories of her beauty and goodness and had longed to lay the best he had at her feet. The princess then took her father into her confidence and begged him to advise her what courtesy she might return to one who persisted in making her such presents.

'Well,' said the king, 'you cannot refuse them; so the best thing you can do is to send this unknown friend at once a present so magnificent that he is not likely to be able to send you anything better, and so will be ashamed to send anything at all!' Then he ordered that, in place of each of the ten horses, two mules laden with silver should be returned by her.

Thus, in a few hours, the merchant found himself in charge of a splendid caravan; and he had to hire a number of armed men to defend it on the road against the robbers. He was glad, indeed, to find himself back again in Wali Dâd's hut.

'Well, now,' cried Wali Dâd, as he viewed all the wealth laid at his door, 'I can well repay that kind prince for his magnificent present of horses. But to be sure you have been put to great expense! Still, if you will accept six mules and their loads, and will take the rest straight to Nekabad, I shall thank you heartily.'

The merchant felt handsomely repaid for his trouble and wondered greatly how the matter would turn out. So he made no difficulty about it, and as soon as he could get ready, he set out for Nekabad with this new and princely gift.

This time the prince, too, was embarrassed and questioned the merchant closely. The merchant felt that his credit was at stake, and while inwardly determining that he would not carry the joke any farther, could not help describing Wali Dâd in such glowing terms that the old man would never have known himself had he heard them.

The prince, like the King of Khaistân, determined that he would send in return a gift that would be truly royal, and which would perhaps prevent the unknown giver sending him anything more. So he made up a caravan of twenty splendid horses caparisoned in gold-embroidered cloths, with fine morocco saddles and silver bridles and stirrups, also twenty camels of the best breed, which had the speed of race horses, and could swing along at a trot all day without getting tired; and, lastly, twenty elephants, with magnificent silver howdahs and coverings of silk embroidered with pearls. To take care of these animals the merchant hired a little army of men, and the troop made a great show as they traveled along.

When Wali Dâd from a distance saw the cloud of dust which the caravan made, and the glitter of its appointments, he said to himself, O Allah! Here's a grand crowd coming! Elephants, too! Grass will be selling well today!' And with that

'O Allah! Here's a grand crowd coming!'

he hurried off to the jungle and cut grass as fast as he could. As soon as he returned he found the caravan had stopped at his door, and the merchant was waiting, a little anxiously, to tell him the news and to congratulate him upon his riches.

'Riches!' cried Wali Dâd. 'What has an old man like me, with one foot in the grave, to do with riches? That beautiful young princess, now! She'd be the one to enjoy all these fine things! Do you take for yourself two horses, two camels, and two elephants, with all their trappings, and present the rest to her.'

The merchant at first objected, and pointed out to Wali Dâd that he was beginning to feel these embassies a little awkward. Of course he was himself richly repaid, so far as expenses went, but still he did not like going so often, and he was getting nervous. At length, however, he consented to go once more, but he promised himself never to embark on another such enterprise.

So, after a few days' rest, the caravan started off once more for Khaistân.

The moment the King of Khaistân saw the gorgeous train of men and beasts entering his palace courtyard, he was so amazed that he hurried down in person to inquire about it and became dumb when he heard that these also were a present from the princely Wali Dâd, and were for the princess, his daughter. He went hastily off to her apartments, and said to her:

'I tell you what it is, my dear, this man wants to marry you, that is the meaning of all these presents! There is nothing for it but that we go and pay him a visit in person. He must be a man of immense wealth, and as he is so devoted to you, perhaps you might do worse than marry him!'

The princess agreed with all that her father said, and orders were issued for vast numbers of elephants and camels, and gorgeous tents and flags, and litters for the ladies, and horses for the men, to be prepared without delay, as the king and princess were going to pay a visit to the great and munificent prince, Wali Dâd. The merchant, the king declared, was to guide the party.

The feelings of the poor merchant in this sore dilemma can hardly be imagined. Willingly would he have run away, but he was treated with so much hospitality as Wali Dâd's representative that he hardly had an instant's real peace and never any opportunity of slipping away. In fact, after a few days, despair possessed him to such a degree that he made up his mind all that had happened was fate and that escape was impossible. But he hoped devoutly some turn of fortune would reveal to him a way out of the difficulties which he had, with the best of intentions, drawn upon himself.

On the seventh day they all started, amidst thunderous salutes from the ramparts of the city, and much dust and cheering and blaring of trumpets.

Day after day they moved on, and every day the poor merchant felt more ill and miserable. He wondered what kind of death the king would invent for him, and went through almost as much torture, as he lay awake nearly the whole of every night thinking over the situation, as he would have suffered if the king's executioners were already setting to work upon him.

At last they were only one day's march from Wali Dâd's little mud home. Here a great encampment was made, and the merchant was sent on to tell Wali Dâd that the King and Princess of Khaistân had arrived and were seeking an interview.

When the merchant arrived he found the poor old man eating his evening meal of onions and dry bread, and when he told him of all that had happened, he had not the heart to proceed to load him with the reproaches which rose to his tongue. For Wali Dâd was overwhelmed with grief and shame for himself, for his friend, and for the name and honor of the princess, and he wept and plucked at his beard and groaned most piteously. With tears he begged the merchant to detain them for one day, by any kind of excuse he could think of, and to come in the morning to discuss what they should do.

As soon as the merchant was gone Wali Dâd made up his mind there was only one honorable way out of the shame and distress he had created by his foolishness, and that was to kill himself. So, without stopping to ask anyone's advice, he went off in the middle of the night to a place where the river wound along at the base of steep rocky cliffs of great height, and determined to throw himself down and put an end to his life. When he reached the place he drew back a few paces, took a little run, and at the very edge of that dreadful black gulf he stopped short! He could not do it!

From below, unseen in the blackness of the deep night shadows, the water roared and boiled round the jagged rocks —he could picture the place as he knew it, only ten times more pitiless and forbidding in the visionless darkness. The wind soughed through the gorge with fearsome sighs and rustlings and whisperings, and the bushes and grasses that grew in the ledges of the cliffs seemed to him like living creatures that danced and beckoned, shadowy and indistinct. An owl laughed 'Hoo! Hoo!' almost in his face, as he peered over the edge of the gulf, and the old man threw himself back in horror. He was afraid! He drew back shuddering, and covering his face in his hands, he wept aloud.

Presently he was aware of a gentle radiance that shed itself before him. Surely morning was not already coming to hasten and reveal his disgrace! He took his hands from before his face and saw before him two lovely beings whom his instinct told him were not mortal, but were peris from paradise.

'Why do you weep, old man?' said one, in a voice as clear and musical as that of the bulbul.

'I weep for shame,' replied he.

'What do you here?' questioned the other.

'I came here to die,' said Wali Dâd. And as they questioned him, he confessed all his story.

Then the first peri stepped forward and laid a hand upon his shoulder, and Wali Dâd began to feel that something strange—what, he did not know—was happening to him. His old cotton rags of clothes were changed to beautiful linen and embroidered cloth, on his hard, bare feet were warm, soft shoes, and on his head a great jeweled turban. Round his neck there lay a heavy golden chain, and the little old bent sickle, with which he cut grass, and which hung from his waistband, had turned into a gorgeous scimitar, its ivory hilt gleaming in the pale light like snow in moonlight.

As he stood wondering, like a man in a dream, the other peri waved her hand and bade him turn and see. And, lo! Before him a noble gateway stood open and up an avenue of giant plane trees the peris led him, dumb with amazement. At the end of the avenue, on the very spot where his hut had stood, a gorgeous palace appeared, ablaze with myriads of lights. Its great porticoes and verandahs were occupied by hurrying servants, and guards paced to and fro and saluted him respectfully as he drew near, along mossy walks and through sweeping grassy lawns where fountains were playing and flowers scented the air. Wali Dâd stood stunned and help-less.

'Fear not,' said one of the peris. 'Go to your house, and learn that Allah rewards the simple-hearted.'

With these words they both disappeared and left him. He walked on, thinking still that he must be dreaming. Very soon he retired to rest in a splendid room, far grander than anything he had ever dreamed of.

When morning dawned he woke and found that the palace and himself and his servants were all real, and that he was not dreaming after all!

If he was dumbfounded, the merchant, who was ushered into his presence soon after sunrise, was much more so. He told Wali Dâd that he had not slept all night, and by the first streak of daylight had started to seek out his friend. And what a search it had been! A great stretch of wild jungle country had, in the night, been changed into parks and gardens; and if it had not been for some of Wali Dâd's new servants, who found him and brought him to the palace, he would have fled away under the impression that his trouble had sent him crazy, and that all he saw was only imagination.

Then Wali Dâd told the merchant all that had happened. By his advice he sent an invitation to the King and Princess of Khaistân to come and be his guests, together with all their retinue and servants, down to the very humblest in the camp.

For three nights and days a great feast was held in honor of the royal guests. Every evening the king and his nobles were served on golden plates and from golden cups; and the smaller people on silver plates and from silver cups; and each evening each guest was requested to keep the plates and cups that they had used as a remembrance of the occasion. Never had anything so splendid been seen. Besides the great dinners, there were sports and hunting, dances and amusements of all sorts.

On the fourth day the King of Khaistân took his host aside and asked him whether it was true, as he had suspected, that he wished to marry his daughter. But Wali Dâd, after thanking him very much for the compliment, said that he had never dreamed of so great an honor, and that he was far too old and ugly for so fair a lady. But he begged the king to stay with him until he could send for the Prince of Nekabad, who was a most excellent, brave and honorable young man, who would surely be delighted to try to win the hand of the beautiful princess.

To this the king agreed, and Wali Dâd sent the merchant to Nekabad, with a number of attendants, and with such handsome presents that the prince came at once, fell head over ears in love with the princess and married her at Wali Dâd's palace, amidst a fresh outburst of rejoicings.

And now the King of Khaistân and the Prince and Princess of Nekabad, went back to their own countries. Wali Dâd lived to a good old age, befriending all who were in trouble and preserving, in his prosperity, the simple-hearted and generous nature that he had when he was only Wali Dâd Gunjay, the grass cutter.

[Told the author by an Indian.]

The Prince and the Three Fates

ONCE UPON A TIME
a little boy was born to a king who ruled over a great country
through which ran a wide river. The king was nearly beside
himself with joy, for he had always longed for a son to inherit
his crown. He sent messages to beg all the most powerful fairies
to come and see this wonderful baby. In an hour or two, so
many were gathered round the cradle, that the child seemed in
danger of being smothered.

The king, who was watching the fairies eagerly, was disturbed to see them look grave. 'Is there anything the matter?'
he asked anxiously.

The fairies looked at him, and all shook their heads at once.

'He is a beautiful boy, and it is a great pity; but what is to
happen will happen,' said they. 'It is written in the books of
fate that he must die, by either a crocodile, a serpent or a
dog. If we could save him we would; but that is beyond our
power.'

And so saying they vanished.

For a time the king stood where he was, horror-stricken at what he had heard. But being of a hopeful nature, he began at once to invent plans to save the prince from the dreadful doom that awaited him. He sent for his master builder and bade him construct a strong castle on the top of a mountain, which should be fitted with the most precious things from the king's own palace and with every kind of toy a child could wish for. He gave the strictest orders that a guard should walk round the castle night and day.

For four or five years the baby lived in the castle alone with his nurses, taking his airings on the broad terraces, which were surrounded by walls, with a moat beneath, and only a draw-bridge to connect them with the outer world.

One day, when the prince was old enough to run quite fast by himself, he looked from the terrace across the moat and saw a little soft, fluffy ball of a dog jumping and playing on the other side. Now, of course, all dogs had been kept from him for fear the fairies' prophecy should come true, and he had never even beheld one before. So he turned to the page, who was walking behind him, and said:

'What is that funny little thing running so fast over there?'

'That is a dog, Prince,' answered the page.

'Well, bring me one like it, and we will see which can run the faster.' And he watched the dog till it had disappeared round the corner.

The page was much puzzled to know what to do. He had strict orders to refuse the prince nothing; yet he remembered the prophecy and felt that this was a serious matter. At last he thought he had better tell the king the whole story and let him decide the question.

'Oh, get him a dog if he wants one,' said the king, 'he will only cry his heart out if he does not have it.' So a puppy was found, exactly like the other; they might have been twins and perhaps they were.

Years went by, and the boy and the dog played together till the boy grew tall and strong. The time came at last when he sent a message to his father, saying:

'Why do you keep me shut up here, doing nothing? I know all about the prophecy that was made at my birth, but I would far rather be killed at once than live an idle, useless life. Give me arms and let me go, I pray you, and my dog too.'

Again the king granted his wishes, and he and his dog were carried in a ship to the other side of the river, which was so broad it might almost have been the sea. A black horse was waiting for him, tied to a tree, and he mounted and rode away wherever his fancy took him, the dog always at his heels. Never was any prince so happy, and he rode and rode till at length he came to a king's palace.

The king who lived in it did not care about looking after his country or seeing that his people lived cheerful and contented lives. He spent his whole time in making riddles and inventing plans which he had much better have let alone. When the young prince reached the kingdom he had just completed a wonderful house for his only child, a daughter. It had seventy windows, each seventy feet from the ground, and he had sent the royal herald round the borders of the neighboring kingdoms to proclaim that whoever could climb up the walls to the window of the princess should win her for his wife.

The fame of the princess' beauty had spread far and wide, and there was no lack of princes who wished to try their fortune. Very funny the palace must have looked each morning, with the dabs of different color on the white marble as the princes climbed the walls. But though some managed to get farther than others, nobody reached anywhere near the top.

They had already been spending several days in this manner when the young prince arrived. As he was pleasant to look upon and civil to talk to, they welcomed him to the house which had been given them, and saw that his bath was properly perfumed after his long journey.

'Where do you come from?' they said at last. 'And whose son are you?'

But the young prince had reasons for keeping his own secret, and he answered, 'My father was master of the horse to the king of my country, and after my mother died he married another wife. At first all went well, but as soon as she had babies of her own she hated me, and I fled lest she should do me harm.'

The hearts of the other young men were touched as they heard this story, and they did everything they could think of to make him forget his past sorrows.

'What are you doing here?' asked the youth one day.

'We spend our whole time climbing up the walls of the palace, trying to reach the windows of the princess,' answered the young men. 'But, as yet, no one has come within ten feet of them.'

'Oh, let me try too!' cried the prince. 'But tomorrow I will wait and see what you do before I begin.'

So the next day he stood where he could watch the young men climb up, and he noted the places on the wall that seemed most difficult and made up his mind that, when his turn came, he would go up some other way.

Day after day he was to be seen watching the wooers till, one morning, he felt he knew the plan of the walls by heart and took his place by the side of the others. Thanks to what he had learned from the failure of the rest, he managed to grasp one little rough projection after another, till at last, to

the envy of his friends, he stood on the sill of the princess'
window. Looking up from below, they saw a white hand
stretched forth to draw him in.

Then one of the young men ran straight to the king's palace,
and said, 'The wall has been climbed, and the prize is won!'

'By whom?' cried the king, starting up from his throne.
'Which of the princes may I claim as my son-in-law?'

'The youth who succeeded in climbing to the princess' window is not a prince at all,' answered the young man. 'He is the
son of the master of the horse to the great king who dwells
across the river, and he fled from his own country to escape
from the hatred of his stepmother.'

At this news the king was very angry, for it had never
entered his head that anyone but a prince would seek to woo
his daughter.

'Let him go back to the land whence he came!' he shouted
in wrath. 'Does he expect me to give my daughter to an exile?'
And he began to smash the drinking vessels in his fury. Indeed,
he quite frightened the young man who ran hastily home to
his friends and told the youth what the king had said.

Now the princess, who was leaning from her window, heard his words and bade the messenger go back to the king her father and tell him that she had sworn a vow never to eat or drink again if the youth was taken from her. The king was more angry than ever, when he received this message, and he ordered his guards to go at once to the palace and put the successful wooer to death. But the princess threw herself between him and his murderers.

'Lay a finger on him and I shall be dead before sunset,' said she. As they saw she meant it, they left the palace and carried the tale to her father.

By this time the king's anger was dying away, and he began to consider what his people would think of him if he broke the promise he had publicly given. So he ordered the princess to be brought before him and the young man also. When they entered the throne room he was so pleased with the noble air of the victor that his wrath quite melted away, and he ran to him and embraced him.

'Tell me who you are,' he said, when he had recovered himself a little, 'for I will never believe that you have not royal blood in your veins.'

The prince still had his reasons for being silent and only told the same story. However, the king had taken such a fancy to the youth that he said no more, and the marriage took place the following day, and great herds of cattle and a large estate were given to the young couple.

AFTER a little while the prince said to his wife, 'My life is in the hands of three creatures—a crocodile, a serpent and a dog.'

'Ah, how rash you are!' cried the princess, throwing her arms round his neck. 'If you know that, how can you have that horrid beast about you? I will give orders to have him killed at once.'

But the prince would not listen to her.

'Kill my dear little dog, who has been my playfellow since he was a puppy?' exclaimed he. 'Oh, never would I allow that.' And all the princess could get from him was a promise he would always wear a sword and have somebody with him when he left the palace.

When the prince and princess had been married a few months, the prince heard that his father was old and ill and longing to have his eldest son by his side again. The young man could not remain deaf to such a message, and he took a tender farewell of his wife and set out on his journey home.

Now when the prince found he was not likely to leave his father's kingdom again, he sent for his wife and bade the messenger tell her that he would await her coming in the town on the banks of the great river. During the weeks that followed, the prince amused himself as best he could, though he counted the minutes to the arrival of the princess, and when she did come, he at once prepared to start for the court.

That very night, however, while he was asleep, the princess noticed something strange in one of the corners of the room. It was a dark patch and seemed, as she looked, to grow longer and longer, and to be moving slowly toward the cushions on which the prince was lying. She shrank in terror but, slight as was the noise, the thing heard it and raised its head to listen. Then she saw it was the long flat head of a serpent, and the recollection of the prophecy rushed into her mind.

Without waking her husband, she glided out of bed, and taking up a heavy bowl of milk, which stood on a table, laid it on the floor in the path of the serpent—for she knew that no serpent in the world can resist milk. She held her breath as the snake drew near and watched it throw up its head again as if it was smelling something nice, while its forked tongue darted out greedily. At length its eyes fell upon the milk and in an instant it was lapping it so fast that it was a wonder the creature did not choke, for it never took its head from the bowl as long as a drop was left. After that it dropped on the ground and slept heavily. This was what the princess had been waiting for, and catching up her husband's sword, she severed the snake's head from its body.

The morning after this adventure the prince and princess set out for the king's palace but found, when they reached it, that he was already dead. They gave him a magnificent burial, and then the prince had to examine the new laws which had been made in his absence and do a great deal of business besides, till he grew quite ill from fatigue and was obliged to go away to one of his palaces on the banks of the river to rest. Here he soon grew better, and began to hunt and to shoot wild duck with his bow, and wherever he went his dog, now grown very old, went with him.

One morning the prince and his dog were out as usual, and in chasing their game they drew near the bank of the river. The prince was running at full speed after his dog when he almost fell over something that looked like a log of wood. To his surprise a voice spoke to him, and he saw that what he had taken for a log was really a crocodile.

'You cannot escape from me,' it was saying; 'I am your fate, and wherever you go, and whatever you do, you will always find me before you. There is only one means of shaking off my power. If you can dig a pit in the dry sand, which will remain full of water, my spell will be broken. If not, death will come to you speedily. I give you this one chance. Now go.'

The young man walked sadly away, and when he reached the palace, he shut himself into his room and for the rest of the day refused to see anyone, even his wife. At sunset, however, as no sound could be heard through the door, the princess grew quite frightened and made such a noise that the prince was forced to draw back the bolt and let her come in.

'How pale you look,' she cried, 'has anything hurt you? Tell me, I pray you, what is the matter, for perhaps I can help!'

So the prince told her the whole story and of the impossible task given him by the crocodile.

'How can a sand hole remain full of water?' asked he. 'Of course it will all run through. The crocodile called it a chance; but he might as well have dragged me into the river at once. He said truly that I cannot escape him.'

'Oh, if that is all,' cried the princess, 'I can set you free myself, for my fairy godmother taught me to know the use of plants, and in the desert not far from here there grows a little four-leaved herb which will keep the water in the pit for a whole year. I will go in search of it at dawn, and you can begin to dig the hole as soon as you like.'

To comfort her husband, the princess had spoken lightly and gaily, but she knew very well she had no light task before her. Still, she was full of courage and energy and determined that, one way or another, her husband should be saved.

It was still starlight when she left the palace on a snow-white donkey and rode away from the river straight to the west. For some time she could see nothing before her but a flat waste of sand, which became hotter and hotter as the sun rose. Then a dreadful thirst seized her and the donkey, but there was no stream to quench it, and if there had been she would hardly have had time to stop. She still had far to go and must be back before evening, else the crocodile might declare that the prince had not fulfilled his conditions. So she spoke cheering words to her donkey, who brayed in reply, and the two pushed steadily on.

Oh, how glad they both were when they caught sight of a tall rock in the distance! They forgot that they were thirsty and the sun hot. The ground seemed to fly under their feet, till the donkey stopped of its own accord in the cool shadow. But though the donkey might rest the princess could not, for she knew the plant grew on the very top of the rock, and a wide chasm ran round the foot of it.

Luckily she had brought a rope with her, and making a noose at one end, she flung it across with all her might. The first time it slid back slowly into the ditch, and she had to draw it up and throw it again, but at length the noose caught on something, the princess could not see what, and she had to trust her whole weight to this little bridge, which might snap and let her fall deep down among the rocks. And in that case her death was as certain as that of the prince.

But nothing so dreadful happened. The princess safely reached the other side, and then came the worst part of her task. As fast as she put her foot on a ledge of rock the stone broke away and left her in the same place as before. Meanwhile the hours were passing and it was nearly noon.

The heart of the poor princess was filled with despair, but she would not give up the struggle. She looked round and saw a small stone above her which seemed rather stronger than the rest, and poising her foot lightly on those that lay between, she managed by a great effort to reach it. With torn and bleeding hands, she gained the top. Here such a violent wind was blowing that, almost blinded with dust, she was obliged to throw herself on the ground and feel about for the precious herb.

For a few terrible moments she thought the rock was bare and her journey had been to no purpose. Feel where she would, there was nothing but grit and stones when, suddenly, her fingers touched something soft in a crevice. It was a plant, that was clear; but was it the right one? See she could not, for the wind was blowing more fiercely than ever, so she lay where she was and counted the leaves. One, two, three—yes! Yes! There were four! And plucking it she held it safe in her hand while she turned, almost stunned by the wind, to go down the rock.

When once she was safely over the side all became still in a moment, and she slid down the rock so fast that it was a wonder she did not land in the chasm. However, by good luck, she stopped quite close to her rope bridge and was soon across it. The donkey brayed joyfully at the sight of her and set off home at his best speed, never seeming to know that the earth under his feet was nearly as hot as the sun above him.

On the bank of the great river he halted, and the princess rushed up to where the prince was standing by the pit he had dug in the dry sand, with a huge water pot beside it. A little way off the crocodile lay blinking in the sun, with his sharp teeth and yellow jaws wide open.

At a signal from the princess the prince poured the water into the hole, and the moment it reached the brim the princess flung in the four-leaved plant. Would the charm work, or would the water trickle away slowly through the sand, and the prince fall a victim to that horrible monster? For half an hour they stood with their eyes fixed on the spot, but the hole remained as full as at the beginning, with the little green leaves floating on the top. Then the prince turned with a shout of triumph, and the crocodile sulkily plunged into the river.

The prince had escaped forever the second of his three fates!

He stood there looking after the crocodile, rejoicing that he was free, when he was startled by a wild duck which flew past them, seeking shelter among the rushes that bordered the edge of the stream. In another instant his dog dashed by in hot pursuit and knocked heavily against his master's legs.

The prince staggered, lost his balance, and fell backward into the river, where the mud and the rushes caught him and held him fast. He shrieked for help to his wife, who came running, and luckily brought her rope with her. The poor old dog was drowned, but the prince was pulled to shore.

'My wife,' he said, 'has been stronger than my fate.'

[Adapted from *Les Contes Populaires de l'Egypte Ancienne*.]

The Boy Who Found Fear

ONCE UPON A TIME there lived a woman who had one son whom she loved dearly. The little cottage in which they dwelt was built on the outskirts of a forest, and as they had no neighbors, the place was very lonely, and the boy was kept at home by his mother to bear her company.

They were sitting together on a winter's evening, when a storm suddenly sprang up, and the wind blew the door open. The woman started and shivered glancing over her shoulder as if she half expected to see some horrible thing behind her.

'Go and shut the door,' she said hastily to her son, 'I feel frightened.'

'Frightened?' repeated the boy. 'What does it feel like to be frightened?'

'Well—just frightened,' answered the mother. 'A fear of something, you hardly know what, takes hold of you.'

'It must be very odd to feel like that,' replied the boy. 'I will go through the world and seek fear till I find it.' And the next morning, before his mother was out of bed, he had left the forest behind him.

After walking for some hours he reached a mountain which he began to climb. Near the top, in a wild and rocky spot, he came upon a band of fierce robbers, sitting round a fire. The boy, who was cold and tired, was delighted to see the bright flames, so he went up to them and said, 'Good greeting to you, sirs,' and wriggled himself in between the men, till his feet almost touched the burning logs.

The robbers stopped drinking and eyed him curiously, and at last the captain spoke.

'No caravan of armed men would dare to come here, even the very birds shun our camp, and who are you to venture in so boldly?'

'Oh, I have left my mother's house in search of fear. Perhaps you can show it to me?'

'Fear is wherever we are,' answered the captain.

'But where?' asked the boy, looking round. 'I see nothing.'

'Take this pot and some flour and butter and sugar over to the churchyard which lies down there, and bake us a cake for supper,' replied the robber.

And the boy, who was by this time quite warm, jumped up cheerfully, and slinging the pot over his arm, ran down the hill. When he came to the churchyard he collected some sticks and made a fire; then he filled the pot with water from a little stream close by, and mixing the flour and butter and sugar together, he set the cake on to cook. It was not long before it grew crisp and brown, and then the boy lifted it from the pot and placed it on a stone, while he put out the fire.

At that moment a hand was stretched from a grave, and a voice said, 'Is that cake for me?'

'Do you think I am going to give to the dead the food of the living?' replied the boy, with a laugh. He gave the hand a tap with his spoon, and picking up the cake, he went up the mountainside, whistling merrily.

'Well, have you found fear?' asked the robbers when he held out the cake to the captain.

'No; was it there?' answered the boy. 'I saw nothing but a hand which came from a grave and belonged to someone who wanted my cake, but I just rapped the fingers with my spoon, and said it was not for him, and then the hand vanished. Oh, how nice the fire is!' And he flung himself on his knees before it, and so did not notice the glances of surprise the robbers cast at each other.

'There is another chance for you,' said one at length. 'On the other side of the mountain lies a deep pool. Go to that, and perhaps you may meet fear on the way.'

'I hope so, indeed,' answered the boy. And he set out at once.

He soon beheld the waters of the pool gleaming in the moonlight, and as he drew near he saw a tall swing standing just over it, and in the swing a child was seated, weeping bitterly.

That is a strange place for a swing, thought the boy; but I wonder what he is crying about. And he was hurrying on toward the child, when a maiden ran up and spoke to him.

'I want to lift my little brother from the swing,' cried she, 'but it is so high above me that I cannot reach. If you will get closer to the edge of the pool, and let me mount on your shoulder, I think I can reach him.'

'Willingly,' replied the boy, and in an instant the girl had climbed to his shoulders. But instead of lifting the child from the swing, as she could easily have done, she pressed her feet so firmly on either side of the youth's neck that he felt in another minute he would be choked or else fall into the water beneath him. So gathering up all his strength, he gave a mighty heave, and threw the girl backward. As she touched the ground a bracelet fell from her arm, and this the youth picked up.

'I may as well keep it as a remembrance of all the queer things that have happened to me since I left home,' he said to himself, and turning to look for the child, he saw that both it and the swing had vanished, and that the first streaks of dawn were in the sky.

With the bracelet on his arm, the youth started for a little town which was situated in the plain on the further side of the mountain, and as, hungry and thirsty, he entered its principal street, a man stopped him. 'Where did you get that bracelet?' asked the man. 'It belongs to me.'

'No, it is mine,' replied the boy.

'It is not. Give it to me at once, or it will be the worse for you!'

'Let us go before a judge, and tell him our stories,' said the boy. 'If he decides in your favor, you shall have it; if in mine, I will keep it!'

To this the man agreed, and the two went together to the great hall, in which the kadi was administering justice. He listened very carefully to what each had to say, and then pronounced his verdict. Neither of the two claimants had proved his right to the bracelet, therefore it must remain in the possession of the judge till its fellow was brought before him.

When they heard this, the man and the boy looked at each other, and their eyes said, 'Where are we to find the other one?' But as they knew there was no use in disputing the decision, they bowed low and left the hall of audience.

WANDERING he knew not whither, the youth found himself on the seashore. At a little distance was a ship which had struck

Down he went, down, down, down!

on a hidden rock and was rapidly sinking, while on deck the
crew were gathered, with faces white as death, shrieking, and
wringing their hands.

'Have you met with fear?' shouted the boy. And the answer
came above the noise of the waves.

'Oh, help! Help! We are drowning!'

Then the boy flung off his clothes, and swam to the ship,
where many hands were held out to draw him on board.

'The ship is tossed hither and thither, and will soon be
sucked down,' cried the crew again. 'Death is very near, and
we are frightened!'

'Give me a rope,' said the boy in reply, and he took it, made
it fast round his body at one end and to the mast at the other,
and sprang into the sea. Down he went, down, down, down,
till at last his feet touched the bottom, and he stood up and
looked about him.

There, sure enough, a sea maiden with a wicked face was
tugging hard at a chain which she had fastened to the ship
with a grappling iron, and was dragging it bit by bit beneath
the waves. Seizing her arms in both his hands, he forced her
to drop the chain, and the ship above remaining steady, the
sailors were able to float her off the rock. Then taking a rusty
knife from a heap of seaweed at his feet, the boy cut the rope
round his waist and fastened the sea maiden firmly to a stone,
so that she could do no more mischief, and bidding her farewell, he swam back to the beach, where his clothes were still
lying.

The youth dressed himself quickly and walked on till he
came to a beautiful shady garden, filled with flowers, and with
a clear little stream running through. The day was hot, and he
was tired, so he entered the gate and seated himself under a

clump of bushes covered with sweet-smelling red blossoms, and it was not long before he fell asleep.

Suddenly a rush of wings and a cool breeze awakened him, and raising his head cautiously, he saw three doves plunging into the stream. They splashed joyfully about, shook themselves, and then dived to the bottom of a deep pool. When they appeared again they were no longer three doves, but three beautiful damsels, bearing between them a table made of mother of pearl. On this they placed drinking cups fashioned from pink and green shells, and one of the maidens filled a cup from a crystal goblet, and was raising it to her mouth, when her sister stopped her.

'To whose health do you drink?' asked she.

'To the youth who prepared the cake and rapped my hand with the spoon when I stretched it out of the earth,' answered the maiden, 'and was never afraid as other men were! But to whose health do you drink?'

'To the youth on whose shoulders I climbed at the edge of the pool, and who threw me off with such a jerk that I lay unconscious on the ground for hours,' replied the second. 'But you, my sister,' added she, turning to the third girl, 'to whom do you drink?'

'Down in the sea I took hold of a ship and shook it and pulled it till it would soon have been lost,' said she. 'But a youth came and freed the ship and bound me to a rock. To his health I drink.' And they all three lifted their cups and drank silently.

As they put their cups down, the youth appeared before them.

'Here am I, the youth whose health you have drunk; and now give me the bracelet that matches a jeweled band which

of a surety fell from the arm of one of you. A man tried to take
it from me, but I would not let him have it, and he dragged
me before the kadi, who kept my bracelet till I could show him
its fellow. And I have been wandering hither and thither in
search of it, and that is how I have found myself in such
strange places.'

'Come with us, then,' said the maidens. They led him down
a passage into a hall, out of which opened many chambers,
each one of greater splendor than the last. From a shelf heaped
up with gold and jewels the eldest sister took a bracelet, which
in every way was exactly like the one which was in the judge's
keeping, and fastened it to the youth's arm.

'Go at once and show this to the kadi,' said she, 'and he will
give you the fellow to it.'

'I shall never forget you,' answered the youth, 'but it may be
long before we meet again, for I shall never rest till I have
found fear.'

Then he went his way and won the bracelet from the kadi.
After this, he again set forth in his quest of fear.

On and on walked the youth, but fear never crossed his path,
and one day he entered a large town, where all the streets and
squares were so full of people, he could hardly pass between
them.

'Why are all these crowds gathered together?' he asked of
a man who stood next him.

'The ruler of this country is dead,' was the reply, 'and as he
had no children, it is needful to choose a successor. Therefore,
each morning, one of the sacred pigeons is let loose from the
tower yonder, and on whomsoever the bird shall perch, that
man is our king. In a few minutes the pigeon will fly. Wait and
see what happens.'

Every eye was fixed on the tall tower which stood in the

center of the chief square, and the moment that the sun was seen to stand straight over it, a door was opened and a beautiful pigeon, gleaming with pink and gray, blue and green, came rushing through the air. Onward it flew, onward, onward, till at length it rested on the head of the boy. Then a great shout arose:

'The king! The king!' But as he listened to the cries, a vision, swifter than lightning, flashed across his mind. He saw himself seated on a throne, spending his life trying, and never succeeding, to make poor people rich; miserable people happy; bad people good; never doing anything he wished to do, not able even to marry the girl that he loved.

'No! No!' he shrieked, hiding his face in his hands. But the crowds who heard him thought he was overcome by the grandeur that awaited him and paid no heed.

'Well, to make quite sure, let fly more pigeons,' said they, but each pigeon followed where the first had led, and the cries arose louder than ever, 'The king! The king!'

And as the young man heard, a cold shiver, that he knew not the meaning of, ran through him.

'This is fear that you have so long sought,' whispered a voice, which seemed to reach his ears alone. And the youth bowed his head as the vision once more flashed before his eyes, and he accepted his doom and made ready to pass his life with fear beside him.

[Adapted from *Türkische Volksmärchen*. Von Dr. Ignas Künos.
E. J. Brill, Leiden.]

The Story of Zoulvisia

IN THE MIDST OF A
sandy desert, in Asia, the eyes of travelers were refreshed by
the sight of a high mountain covered with beautiful trees,
among which the glitter of foaming waterfalls might be seen
in the sunlight. In that clear, still air it was even possible to
hear the song of the birds, and smell of the flowers; but though
the mountain was plainly inhabited—for here and there a
white tent was visible—none of the kings or princes who passed
it on the road to Babylon or Baalbec ever plunged into its
forests—or, if they did, they never came back. Indeed, so great
was the terror caused by the evil reputation of the mountain
that fathers, on their deathbeds, prayed their sons never to try
to fathom its mysteries. But in spite of its ill fame, a certain
number of young men every year announced their intention of
visiting it and were never seen again.

Now there was once a powerful king who ruled over a
country on the other side of the desert, and when dying, he
gave the usual counsel to his seven sons. Hardly, however, was
he dead than the eldest, who succeeded to the throne, declared
he would hunt in the enchanted mountain. In vain the old men
shook their heads and tried to persuade him to give up his mad

scheme. All was useless. He went, but did not return; and in due time the throne was filled by his next brother.

And so it happened to the other five, but when the youngest became king, and he also proclaimed a hunt in the mountain, a loud lament was raised in the city.

'Who will reign over us when you are dead? For dead you surely will be!' cried they. 'Stay with us, and we will make you happy.' For a while he listened to their prayers, and the land grew rich and prosperous under his rule. But in a few years the restless fit again took possession of him, and this time hunt in that forest he would. Calling his friends and attendants round him, he set out one morning across the desert.

They were riding through a rocky valley, when a deer sprang up in front of them and bounded away. The king instantly gave chase, followed by his attendants; but the animal ran so swiftly that they never could catch up with it, and at length it vanished in the depths of the forest.

When the young man drew rein for the first time and looked about him, he found he had left his companions far behind. Glancing back, he beheld them entering some tents, dotted here and there amongst the trees. For himself, the fresh coolness of the woods was more attractive to him than any food, however delicious, and for hours he strolled about as his fancy led him.

By-and-by it began to grow dark, and he thought they should start for the palace. So, leaving the forest with a sigh, he made his way down to the tents, but what was his horror to find his men lying about, some dead, some dying. All were past speech, but speech was needless. It was as clear as day the wine they had drunk contained deadly poison.

'I am too late to help you, my poor friends,' he said, gazing at them sadly; 'but at least I can avenge you! Those who have set the snare will certainly return to see to its working. I will hide myself and discover who they are!'

Near the spot he saw a large walnut tree, and into this he climbed. Night soon fell, and nothing broke the stillness of the place; but with the earliest glimpse of dawn a noise of galloping hoofs was heard.

Pushing the branches aside the young man beheld a youth approaching, mounted on a white horse. On reaching the tents the cavalier dismounted and closely inspected the dead bodies that lay about. Then, one by one, he dragged them to a ravine close by and threw them into a lake at the bottom. While he was doing this, the servants who had followed him led away the horses of the ill-fated men, and the courtiers were ordered to let loose the deer, which was used as a decoy, and to see that the tables in the tents were covered as before with food and wine.

Having made these arrangements the youth strolled slowly through the forest, but great was his surprise to come upon a beautiful horse hidden in the depths of a thicket.

'There was a horse for every dead man,' he said to himself. 'Then whose is this?'

'Mine,' answered a voice from a walnut tree close by. 'Who are you that lure men into your power and then poison them? But you shall do so no longer. Return to your house, wherever it may be, and we will fight before it!'

The cavalier was speechless with anger at these words; then with a great effort he replied:

'I accept your challenge. Mount and follow me. I am Zoulvisia.' And springing on his horse, he was out of sight so quickly that the king had only time to notice that light seemed to flow from himself and his steed, and that the hair under his helmet was like liquid gold.

Clearly, the cavalier was a woman. But who could she be?
Was she queen of all the queens? Or was she chief of a band
of robbers? He took the path down which the rider had gone,
and rode along it for many hours till he came to three huts
side by side, in each of which lived an old fairy and her sons.

The poor king was by this time so tired and hungry he
could hardly speak, but when he had drunk some milk, and
rested a little, he was able to reply to the questions they eagerly
put to him.

'I am going to seek Zoulvisia,' said he. 'She has slain my
brothers and many of my subjects, and I mean to avenge them.'

He had only spoken to the inhabitants of one house, but from
all three came an answering murmur.

'What a pity we did not know! Twice this day has she passed
our door and we might have kept her prisoner.'

But though their words were brave their hearts were not, for
the mere thought of Zoulvisia made them tremble.

'Forget Zoulvisia, and stay with us,' they all said, holding
out their hands. 'You shall be our big brother and we will be
your little brothers.' But the king would not stay.

Drawing from his pocket a pair of scissors, a razor and a
mirror, he gave one to each of the old fairies, saying:

'Though I may not give up my vengeance I accept your
friendship, and therefore leave you these three tokens. If blood
should appear on the face of any know that my life is in danger
and, in memory of our sworn brotherhood, come to my aid.'

'We will come,' they answered. And the king mounted his
horse and set out along the road they showed him.

By the light of the moon presently he saw a splendid palace,
but though he rode twice round it, he could find no door. He
was considering what he should do next, when he heard the
sound of loud snoring, which seemed to come from his feet.

Looking down, he beheld an old man lying at the bottom of a deep pit, just outside the walls, with a lantern by his side.

Perhaps he may be able to give me some counsel, thought the king; and with some difficulty, he scrambled into the pit and laid his hand on the shoulder of the sleeper.

'Are you a bird or a snake that you can enter here?' asked the old man, awakening with a start.

But the king answered that he was a mere mortal and that he sought Zoulvisia.

'Zoulvisia? The world's curse?' replied the old man, gnashing his teeth. 'Out of all the thousands she has slain I am the only one who has escaped, though why she spared me only to condemn me to this living death I cannot guess.'

'Help me if you can,' said the king. And he told the old man his story.

'Take heed then to my counsel,' answered the old man who had listened intently. 'Know that every day at sunrise Zoulvisia dresses herself in her jacket of pearls and mounts the steps of her crystal watch tower. From there she can see all over her lands and behold the entrance of either man or demon. If so much as one is detected she utters such fearful cries that those who hear her die of fright. But hide yourself in a cave that lies near the foot of the tower and plant a forked stick in front of it. When she has uttered her third cry, go forth boldly, and look up at the tower. And go without fear, for you will have broken her power.'

The king did exactly what the old man had bidden him, and when he stepped forth from the cave, their eyes met.

'You have conquered me and broken the evil enchantment,' said Zoulvisia. 'You are worthy to be my husband, for you are the first man who has not died at the sound of my voice!' Letting down her golden hair, she drew up the king to the

Suddenly a fine stag started up

crystal watch tower as with a rope. Then she led him into the hall of audience and presented him to her household.

'Ask of me what you will, and I will grant it to you,' whispered Zoulvisia, with a smile, as they sat together on a mossy bank by the stream. And the king prayed her to set free the old man to whom he owed his life, and to send him back to his own country.

'I HAVE finished with hunting, and with riding about my lands,' said Zoulvisia, the day they were married. 'The care of providing for us belongs henceforth to you.' And turning to her attendants, she bade them bring the horse of fire before her.

'This is your master, oh, my steed of flame,' cried she; 'you will serve him as you have served me.' And kissing the horse between his eyes, she placed the bridle in the hand of her husband.

The horse looked for a moment at the young man, and then bent his head, while the king patted his neck and smoothed his tail, till they felt themselves old friends. After this he mounted to do Zoulvisia's bidding, but before he started she gave him a case of pearls containing one of her hairs, which he tucked into the breast of his coat.

He rode along for some time, without seeing any game to bring home for dinner. Suddenly a fine stag started up almost under his feet, and he at once gave chase. On they sped, but the stag twisted and turned till they reached a broad river, when the animal jumped in and swam across. The king fitted his cross-bow with a bolt, and took aim, but though he succeeded in wounding the stag, it contrived to gain the opposite bank, and in his excitement he never observed that the case of pearls had fallen into the water.

The stream, though deep, was likewise rapid, and the box

was swirled along miles and miles and miles, till it was washed
up in quite another country, where it was picked up by one of
the water-carriers belonging to the palace, who showed it to
the king. The workmanship of the case was so curious, and the
pearls so rare, the king could not make up his mind to part
with it. He gave the man a good price and sent him away
Then. summoning his chamberlain, he bade him find out its
history in three days or lose his head.

But the answer to the riddle, which puzzled all the magicians
and wise men, was given by an old woman, who came up to
the palace and told the chamberlain that, for two handfuls of
gold. she would reveal it.

Of course the chamberlain gladly gave her what she asked,
and in return she informed him that the case and the hair
belonged to Zoulvisia.

'Bring her hither, old crone, and you shall have gold enough
to stand up in,' said the chamberlain. And the old woman
answered she would try what she could do.

She went back to her hut in the middle of the forest, and
standing in the doorway, whistled softly. Soon the dead leaves
on the ground began to move and to rustle, and from underneath them there came a long train of serpents. They wriggled
to the feet of the witch, who stooped down and patted their
heads. She gave each one some milk in a red earthen basin.
When they had all finished, she whistled again, and bade two
or three coil themselves round her arms and neck, while she
turned one into a cane and another into a whip. Then she took
a stick, and on the river bank changed it into a raft, and seating
herself comfortably, she pushed off into the center of the
stream.

All that day she floated, and all the next night, and toward
sunset the following evening she found herself close to Zoul-

visia's garden, just at the moment that the king, on the horse of flame, was returning from hunting.

'Who are you?' he asked in surprise. 'Who are you, and why have you come here?'

'I am a poor pilgrim, my son,' answered she, 'and having missed the caravan, I have wandered foodless for many days through the desert, till at length I reached the river. There I found this tiny raft, and to it I committed myself, not knowing if I should live or die. But since you have found me, give me I pray you bread to eat, and let me lie this night by the dog who guards your door!'

This piteous tale touched the heart of the young man.

'Mount behind me, good woman,' cried he, 'for you have walked far, and it is still a long way to the palace.' And as he spoke he bent down to help her, but the horse swerved to one side.

And so it happened twice and thrice, and the old witch guessed the reason, though the king did not.

'I fear to fall off,' said she; 'but as your kind heart pities my sorrows, ride slowly, and lame as I am, I think I can manage to keep up.'

At the door he bade the witch to rest herself, and he would fetch her all she needed. But Zoulvisia, his wife, grew pale when she heard whom he had brought, and besought him to feed the old woman and send her away, as she would cause mischief to befall them.

The king laughed at her fears, and answered lightly, 'Why, one would think she was a witch to hear you talk! And even if she were, what harm could she do to us?' Calling to the maidens he bade them carry her food and to let her sleep in their chamber.

Now the old woman was very cunning and kept the maidens

awake half the night with all kinds of strange stories. Next morning, while they were dressing their mistress, one of them suddenly broke into a laugh, in which the others joined her.

'What is the matter with you?' asked Zoulvisia. The maid answered that she was thinking of a droll adventure told them by the old woman.

'Oh, madam,' cried the girl, 'it may be that she is a witch, as they say; but I am sure she never would work a spell to harm a fly! And as for her tales, they would pass many a dull hour for you, when my lord was absent!'

So, in an evil hour, Zoulvisia consented that the crone should be brought to her, and from that moment the two were hardly ever apart.

ONE day the witch began to talk about the young king, and to declare that in all the lands she had visited she had seen none like him. 'It was so clever of him to guess your secret so as to win your heart,' said she. 'And of course he told you his, in return?'

'No, I don't think he has any,' returned Zoulvisia.

'Not have any secrets?' cried the old woman scornfully. 'That is nonsense! Every man has a secret, which he always tells to the woman he loves. And if he has not told it to you, it is because he does not love you!'

These words troubled Zoulvisia though she would not confess it to the witch. But the next time she found herself alone with her husband, she began to coax him to tell her in what lay the secret of his strength. For a long while he put her off with caresses, but when she would be no longer denied, he answered:

'It is my saber that gives me strength, and day and night it lies by my side. Now that I have told you, swear upon this ring, that I will give you in exchange for yours, that you will reveal it to nobody.'

And Zoulvisia did so, and instantly hastened to betray the great news to the old woman.

Four nights later, when all the world was asleep, the witch crept softly into the king's chamber and took the saber from his side as he lay sleeping. Then, opening her lattice, she flew on to the terrace and dropped the sword into the river.

The next morning everyone was surprised because the king did not, as usual, rise early to hunt. The attendants listened at the keyhole and heard the sound of heavy breathing, but none dared enter, till Zoulvisia pushed past. And what a sight met their gaze! There lay the king almost dead, with foam on his mouth, and eyes that were already closed. They wept, and they cried to him, but no answer came.

Suddenly a shriek broke from those who stood hindmost, and in strode the witch, with serpents round her neck and arms and hair. At a sign from her they flung themselves with a hiss upon the maidens, whose flesh was pierced with their poisonous fangs. Then turning to Zoulvisia, she said:

'I give you your choice—will you come with me or shall the serpents slay you also?' And as the terrified girl stared at her, unable to utter one word, she seized her by the arm and led her to the place where the raft was hidden among the rushes. Then they floated down the stream till they had reached the neighboring country, where Zoulvisia was sold for a sack of gold to the king.

Now, since the young man had entered the three huts on his way through the forest, not a morning had passed without the sons of the three fairies examining the scissors, the razor and the mirror, which the young king had left with them. Hitherto the surfaces of all three things had been bright and undimmed, but on this particular morning, when they took them out as usual, drops of blood stood on the razor and the scissors, while the little mirror was clouded over.

'Something terrible must have happened to our big brother,' they whispered to each other, with awestruck voices. 'We must hasten to his rescue ere it be too late.' And putting on their magic slippers they started for the palace.

The servants greeted them eagerly, ready to pour forth all they knew, but that was not much; only that the saber had vanished, none knew where. The little men passed the whole of the day in searching for it, but it could not be found, and when night closed in, they were very tired and hungry. But how were they to get food? The king had not hunted that day, and there was nothing for them to eat. The little men were in despair, when a ray of the moon suddenly lit up the river.

'How stupid! Of course there are fish to catch,' cried they. Soon they succeeded in landing some fine fish, which they cooked on the spot. Then they felt better and began to look about them.

Farther out, in the middle of the stream, there was a strange splashing, and by-and-by the body of a huge fish appeared, turning and twisting as if in pain. The eyes of all the brothers were fixed on the spot, when the fish leaped in the air, and a bright gleam flashed through the night. 'The saber!' they shouted, and plunged into the stream, and with a sharp tug pulled out the sword, while the fish lay on the water, exhausted by its struggles. Swimming back with the saber to land, they carefully dried it on their coats, and then carried it to the palace and placed it on the king's pillow. In an instant color came back to the waxen face, and the hollow cheeks filled out. The king sat up, and opening his eyes, he said:

'Where is Zoulvisia?'

'That is what we do not know,' answered the little men; 'but now that you are saved you will soon find out.' And they told him what had happened since Zoulvisia had betrayed his secret to the witch.

'Let me go to my horse,' was all he said. But when he entered the stable he could have wept at the sight of his favorite steed, which was nearly in as sad a plight as his master had been. Languidly he turned his head as the door swung back on its hinges, but when he beheld the king he rose up and rubbed his head against him.

'Oh, my poor horse! How much more clever you were than I! If I had understood you I should never have lost Zoulvisia; but we will seek her together, you and I.'

For a long while the king and his horse followed the course of the stream, but nowhere could he learn anything of Zoulvisia. At length, one evening, they stopped to rest by a cottage not far from a great city. As the king was lying outstretched on the grass, lazily watching his horse cropping the short turf, an old woman came out with a wooden bowl of fresh milk, which she offered him.

He drank it eagerly, for he was very thirsty, and then laying down the bowl began to talk to the woman, who was delighted to have someone listen to her.

'You are in luck to have passed this way just now,' said she, 'for in five days the king holds his wedding banquet. Ah, but the bride is unwilling. Her blue eyes are cast down and her golden hair loosed! She keeps by her side a cup of poison that she will swallow rather than become his wife. Yet he is a handsome man too, and a proper husband for her—more than she could have looked for, having come no one knows whither, and bought from a witch—'

The king started. Had he found his wife after all? His heart beat violently, as if it would choke him; but he gasped out:

'Is her name Zoulvisia?'

'Ay, so she says, though the old witch— But what ails you?' she broke off, as the young man sprang to his feet and seized her wrists.

'Listen to me,' he said. 'Can you keep a secret?'

'Ay,' answered the old woman again, 'if I am paid for it.'

'Oh, you shall be paid, never fear—as much as your heart can desire! Here is a handful of gold: you shall have as much again if you will do my bidding.'

The old crone nodded her head.

'Then go and buy a dress such as ladies wear at court, and manage to gain admittance into the palace and into the presence of Zoulvisia. Show her this ring, and after that she will tell you what to do.'

So the old woman set off, clothed herself in a garment of yellow silk, and wrapped a veil closely round her head. In this dress she walked boldly up the palace steps behind some merchants whom the king had ordered to bring presents for Zoulvisia.

At first the bride would have nothing to say to any of them, but on perceiving the ring, she suddenly grew as meek as a lamb. Thanking the merchants for their trouble, she sent them away, and remained alone with her visitor.

'Grandmother,' asked Zoulvisia, as soon as the door was safely shut, 'where is the owner of this ring?'

'In my cottage,' answered the old woman, 'waiting for orders from you.'

'Tell him to remain there for three days. Now go to the king of this country and say that you have succeeded in bringing me to reason. Then he will let me alone and will cease to watch me. On the third day from this I shall be wandering about the garden near the river, and there your guest will find me. The rest concerns myself only.'

THE morning of the third day dawned, and with the first rays of the sun a bustle began in the palace, for that evening the king was to marry Zoulvisia. Tents were being erected of fine scarlet cloth, decked with wreaths of sweet-smelling white flowers, and in them the banquet was spread. When all was ready a procession was formed to fetch the bride, who had been wandering in the palace gardens since daylight, and crowds lined the way to see her pass. A glimpse of her dress of golden gauze might be caught, as she passed from one flowery thicket to another; then suddenly the multitude swayed, and shrank back, as a thunderbolt seemed to flash out of the sky to the place where Zoulvisia was standing. Ah! But it was no thunderbolt, only the horse of fire! And when the people looked again, it was bounding away with two persons on its back.

Zoulvisia and her husband both learned how to keep happiness when they had it; and that is a lesson many men and women never learn at all. And besides, it is a lesson nobody can teach, and that every boy and girl must learn for themselves.

[From *Contes Arméniens*. Par Louis Macler.]